I0760785

The Chinaberry Tree

Winner
International Impact Book Award

Finalist
American Fiction Award

Winner
Royal Dragonfly Book Award

"... sympathetic evocation of life's randomness, desperateness, pain and beauty ..."

- Dr. Loretta S. Burns, Professor Emerita
Tuskegee University

" ... engaging and memorable ...."

- Dr. Trudier Harris, Professor Emerita
University of Alabama

"Rich with vital voices, spiritual undertones, and urgent cultural and historical insight."

- BookLife/Publishers Weekly

"Brilliant, biting, and deeply human ... The Chinaberry Tree floored me."

- Reedsy Discovery

"... the soul of the book lies in its refusal to sanitize the truth."

- The Valley Weekly

"The lyf so short, the craft so long to lerne ..."

- Chaucer

" ... You have no friends."

- John Henrik Clarke

" ... It has to be the most *under*-hyped book ..."

- Reedsy Discovery

The Chinaberry Tree

A Novel

Jerome Saintjones

STILLMAN HILL PRESS
New York, NY

This is a work of fiction. While certain historical events, locations, and public figures are referenced or depicted in this novel, the story, characters, and specific interactions are products of the author's imagination. Any resemblance to actual persons, living or dead, outside of those explicitly referenced as historical figures, is purely coincidental. The portrayal of historical events and figures has been fictionalized for narrative purposes, and creative liberties have been taken.

Content Disclaimer:
This novel may contain, for some readers, strong language, graphic violence, mature themes, and explicit content. *Reader discretion is advised.*

 Published in the United States of America by
Stillman Hill Press
2248 Broadway #1573
New York, NY 10024
Mailing Address: P.O. Box 1, Normal, AL 35762

Cover design concept developed with assistance from ChatGPT, an AI language model created by OpenAI, based on specific wording and description received from the author.

PARTIAL CATALOGUING INFO:
Names: Saintjones, Jerome, 1959 - author.
Title: The chinaberry tree : a novel / Jerome Saintjones
Description: First edition | New York : Stillman Hill Press
Identifiers: ISBN 978-1-966519-01-0 (paperback)
ISBN 978-1-966519-00-3 (hardback)
ISBN 978-1-966519-02-7 (ebook)

MANUFACTURED IN THE UNITED STATES OF AMERICA

10 9 8 7 6 5 4 3 2 1

First Edition

For Love and Life:
Marilyn and Morgan

For My Eternal Muse:
Loretta S. Burns, Ph.D.

For Friends Indeed:
Dorothy and Georgia

For Ardent Supporters:
Dr. Trudier Harris and Dr. Allen P. Vital

and

For the Ultimate "Gate-Opener":
Jessie Redmon Fauset

The Chinaberry Tree

Chapter 1

At 3:37 a.m., seemingly just this morning, I awake from a dream of 21 Nubian phalluses suspended between two dark caverns. I sit up in the bed, almost levitating, wondering if I'm going crazy or if I'd simply become a pale slave to The Chinaberry Tree and its endless, twisted branches. Only I'm not *really* awake. I'm dreaming that I'm analyzing a dream that isn't quite over.

My brain relieves itself of my skull, pulling away from its Newgrange, then transforming into a pulsating continent of Africa and slowly, so slowly, spinning toward the apex of some cold, dismal ceiling in 19th-century Germany. In the room below it are 14 mainly European men, seven with shining silver sabers, severing a pure Ethiopian princess into seven parts, beginning in the jungle of her Nile, ripping flesh and the last of Eden with it. Her eyes are closed in noble pain, but as the swords reach her golden breasts, the lids flash open and stare at me. My head begins to whirl. Counterclockwise, so does the room, taking with it space and time, as well as sanity, what once was and what now seems to be. The beautiful, soulful brown eyes, too, spin uncontrollably as their tears find their way into my chest and begin to burn there like a magical bush in ancient Kemet. But her ancient and futuristic eyes rise upward, as they must, like a proud religious experience, refusing to dignify King James. They rise to the heavens and then gradually return to earth in their very own upper room.

I'm staring at them now, those beautiful brown eyes. To confuse me, they have divided themselves into several pairs. Simultaneously, all the brown eyes in the place start to work me over, as if I was a cheap thrill at a once-popular house of ill repute, some round and gyrating, impeccably ample rear end, perfectly designed for the best lap dance of the evening. These eyes—transcending past and present, reality and dream—now only await my answer with gut-tightening anticipation. They are lustful in their taking in, yet venomously vicious in their giving out. It is as if my true citizenship, my very sense of belonging—even after all this time—now hinged upon how I sculpted my words. I had worked too damned hard, had listened too well, and had come too far to get to this sorry point. This town belonged to me as much as it did to any of these eyes, including the stoic brown, golden brown and very brown faces sitting in the room, all—*all!*—judging me.

So many times I had talked to these sojourners in some booth in the dark corners of this bar, where they humored me with their stories and I prodded them on, taking in all—at least to the extent of my liver. True, there were too many times when I had fallen into a drunken stupor, only to be shaken by black hands extending deep into my lucid, vivid, white-tormented dreamscape.

Yet in this very instant, I want as much to say, "Kiss my white ass," as I do, "Let's just move on." But, the period I had desperately hoped would be a fleeting moment merely draped the room in a mahogany forever. Is this happening? Has this already happened? Will it happen in the next minute? Oh, what a world of African faces—some wise, some kind and concerned, some unquestionably angry. Still, there were other sets of noble eyes, affixed in the sockets of dazed warriors, trying to regain their bearings as they stared at me. I felt colonized. A limp specimen under a microscope, helpless to an erect light hung perpendicular over my head with a UFO's laser beam under my ass.

I had been brought up believing that all people were to be respected and appreciated for their differences. And, even in the *Book of Common Prayer*, the spirit of cultural and spiritual tolerance was vividly plain, despite the fact that there were few black people in the pews. So, Episcopalians don't recruit. Sue me.

When I was in junior high, I had a black friend ... Gray. He was smart, too. He knew all about the popular rock acts of the day and who were in the bands, like Uriah

Heep, Black Sabbath and Aerosmith. Most of the time, Gray would outscore me on tests in science class. All the time, he would outrun me on the track. Although he was only around fourteen or fifteen, his body was already muscular, and the first signs of a beard and moustache were settling around his chin and upper lip.

During the lunch recess, we would join a group of guys to form two teams. Someone would crush an empty half-pint milk carton into a ball, and we would knock it back and forth between the teams. The team whose member missed the ball or knocked it out of bounds lost the round. One day, Gray was missing. He was so good at the hand-ball game that his absence was immediate. We continued to play, when I noticed Gray walking around the corner of the building. Just as he turned to join us, Judy Ischenbaum came from around the corner, planted a quick kiss on his cheek, and sped back around the corner out of view, deceptively coy.

"Ooh," the boys chimed. "Gray and Ju-dee. Gray and Ju-dee." Gray just smiled. When he eventually looked over at me, he sort of dropped his eyes. He *knew* I had this thing for Judy. I just never got around to making any move. Hell, I was just a teen, too. I was about to let it go, but then one of the guys started teasing Gray.

"Hey, Gray ... gonna get that Jooty booty?" Usually, Gray was cool about such things. I expected him to say, "Naw, man. It's not like that." But he instead reached into his right pants pocket and pulled out a $20 bill.

"Who knows?" he said, with a devilish smile. "She's already paid for it." Perhaps that was when I lost it. Too many images. Too much pain. Too much brown, with thrusting pistons and cylinders and kinky-haired phalluses pushing in and out of things in which they did not belong. How could this liver-lip monkey have thought Judy could ever be his? How could he have thought it *okay* to claim something that did not belong to his kind? Dad might have called her a little Jew, but she was still mostly *our* people.

***

"*Our* people?" Bo Willie had asked me. His words had hit me so hard that I had traveled to prehistoric Ireland, then soared throughout pre-colonial Europe and back again. He wore a fitted black t-shirt with a gold necklace that punctuated his chest with its much-too-large brass "W". His shaved head was a combination of solemnity and old-school thug life, all tightly wrapped together behind a forehead ridged by seven parallel lines, perched above eyes of pure, unapologetic soul. He sat on a table in the open seating area of the bar, a spot meticulously chosen for its power and Eurocentrically perfect for being in the center of Hell. And, when Willie was on his soapbox, which was most of the time, the twelve or so disciples present at any particular time and seated along the long bar, had to swivel around to meet the sound of his voice.

The thunderous Nubian bass bounced about the barroom and now met my ears with a force I had only witnessed directed at others. Bo Willie removed himself from the table and pulled a stool away from the bar. This was, I had learned as a lone white man in a totally black setting, a sign of permanency, of fortitude, of positioning to jump dead into someone's ass. He wore slightly faded black denim jeans and had a tendency to, like a few of his kind do, constantly pull at a bulge in his crotch that should have been massive from all the yanking, if not merely from his perspective.

His was a simple question, but deceptively so. Truth be told, it was an unexpected punch that sent me on another cerebral spiral of time travel. I knew that time actually had stood still, all while my mind was racing madly about, exploring all ancient and current possibilities and outcomes. A wooly-headed Joshua had urged the heavens to hold the sun in its place. The maddening process of thinking had become sheer hell. Should I play it cool? Or, should I show this Bo Willie, his partner-in-crime Brad and that juvenile delinquent Baggy Pants that I am a man, too, and refuse to go down for the count? Yet the notion of standing up in defiance vanished as quickly as it had come. I thought about the importance of the question—"*Our* people?"

That so much rested on it made me angry inside. I was even more pissed that this question was formed by one with such a minute brain. I really loved this town and didn't want some little oral mishap to mess things up.

Funny. Almost at once, the town of Ebonia had intrigued me, from the time I parked on the edge of the small black college campus that bears its name to three years later as a member of the faculty. It also was the captivating backdrop out of which came the two dozen or so men and women who frequented The Chinaberry Tree Bar on my after-class visits. Ebonia was a pathetically small community, not much to visit in terms of fulfilling a longing for entertainment or good food or scenery, for that matter. Perhaps it was something about the people, the way they had gathered in this little black college town from the far reaches of the world. It was almost as if they all had gone on a pilgrimage, only to discover, at various points in their lives and journeys, this remote piece of heaven and hell and had decided to stake their dreams here.

Ebonia maintains its pull on a certain type of people, and I had begun to think I had become precisely that type. I—a man who had never really learned to place much faith in the Nubian mystique, owing primarily to my upbringing—had even scoffed at many of the "educated" blacks in settings like these. I also had secretly hoped never to allow myself to become so careless as to be found out.

Then, after completing my undergraduate and master's degrees at so-called flagship institutions, sheltered from and invisible to this darker world, and after many an intimate evening with some interesting brown sugars, I was finally beginning to see the error of my ways. Soon, I would also be completing requirements for a doctorate degree from the huge predominantly white state university in the neighboring city of Saxonville, just 20 miles away.

***

It was in Ebonia that my education—my quest—to learn

what it was really like to be a black man, really started. It was here that, for the first time, I found myself admiring the ones I had pitied. Soon, I began to willingly trust and demand black doctors, pharmacists, lawyers and even politicians. I finally realized that they were an ancient part of me and that all this time I had been living as a transparent shell. Perhaps more importantly, I came to realize that I was rightly a part of them. It was indeed my heritage.

Little Ebonia could make you proud, yes. Witnessing formerly and currently oppressed people carrying on in their little slice of the world is a sight indeed. Seeing a minority performing as a majority, in majority positions, with majority voices, mannerisms and lifestyles is something to behold. I had learned to celebrate my heritage. *For Africa!*

This is partly the reason why the stares from all the brown eyes so unnerved me. I had made so much progress. Surely, they would not let one slip of the tongue stand in the way of all we had meant to each other. I was one of *them*, dammit! I know this town, like the back of my hand. I know all about the people, their pride and their filth. I have been like an onion, with layers upon layers of accommodation, and have in only three short years learned about the nuances of this town that many would have taken an entire lifetime to learn.

Through quiet observation from my corner of the bar at The Chinaberry Tree, I had learned of The Rift. I know, for instance, that even now, a surprisingly large percentage of educated blacks live in Ebonia, perhaps to a fault.

Nowhere else in the country is there a more heavily concentrated, educated black population per capita, particularly in the above-forty age range. But this sect is both a hellified and glorified group. It has to be the wisest, most opinionated, honest, corrupt, virtuous, sodomic, Afrocentric, Eurocentric, benevolent and downright stubborn lot in American society. Indeed, it also represents the most damnable dichotomy known to man.

On one hand, Ebonians are the type of people destroyed by Noah's flood, the ones who shouted "Crucify Him!" and the ones who discounted the wheel because it wasn't their idea. They are the kind of people you don't turn your back on, the kind you pass blankly on any busy sidewalk, and the kind that rarely make contributions toward the development of a better world. I guess that, in a sense, makes them very much like most of the other people in the world. Yet, when they are operating at their best, they masterfully manage the political, economic and social sectors to no parallel.

Through my personal evening encounters, I also learned that on the social scene Ebonia's elite divided their thumbnail community into the "Have Degrees" and the "Have Not Degrees." Even the Have Degrees were then further divided according to the rank of the degree. Further, unwritten, unspoken law, according to where the degree was earned or whether doctoral sheepskin read "philosophy" or "education," created a caste system within the Have Degrees category.

How dare these guys try to single me out as though I

were some alien life form! I know about all of their monkey shit! I have picked up enough smut about their personal lives to smear their brown noses in muck for a long, long time. They don't want to fuck with me!

Besides, history shows that there has always been division in our societies. Hell, there's a market for it. Ebonia, I had come to know, was simply a sliver of the larger pie under a microscope. Many of its citizens really needed adequate distance between themselves and other people, and yet they yearned for the comity of association. They even needed someone like me for occasional affirmation.

***

You can learn a lot about people by sitting quietly and simply listening, rather than shooting your damn mouth off ... or getting too drunk at The Chinaberry Tree to keep it all tied together. Still, some of the bastards eyeing me now need to learn this. Quit staring at me! You all ain't about shit, either!

Ha! What do you have to say about that? Okay, you smug black asses. I can go some places you really don't want me to go. Like, why is it that Ebonia blacks with lighter complexions dominate the social scene, while the ambitious "darkies" are still fighting for acceptance in the new millennium? Whoo-hoo! Now ain't that some shit for your black intellectual asses? Oops! I know: I shouldn't have gone there. It's a road trip everyone wants to ignore, but one no one has.

News flash, Bo Willie! Somewhere along the line the

intellectual elite in Ebonia has become void of its sense of community. Without that, even the most Christian mother cannot possibly view your child as her own. You people just can't get it together!

So you guys want to judge me, huh? I don't need this from you! I can pack my shit and hit the road tomorrow. And it has nothing to do with the cost of living or what I am or am not getting paid on my little side job teaching at that little college. I'm leaving because of the high cost of saving one's sanity—my own. You're only sane when you're able to see and recognize what is happening to you and to tell yourself that you have some control over it all. I have control, baby! To hell with all of y'all! I'm out of here. In the wind, my friend; so long, I'm gone!

On second thought: I ain't going no damn where! You tree-climbing apes had better back off! I'm staying! Eat me raw! This has nothing to do with my relationships with people, because, surprisingly, the rest of this town accepts me with open arms. I know this. No, I'm not drunk. I can walk in and out of any place I want. I'm white. It's you sick asses who are trying to make *me* a victim. I don't do the victim act, see? I victimize and I prophesy. In fact, I see the likely opening of several cans of black whipass!

***

All of these thoughts and dares kept rushing through my mind at such speed that I felt even more dizzy. They were daggers that ripped apart my flesh one mid-March evening. It had finally come. That fateful day when my delusions came crashing down on me all in an instant. The people from whom I had learned so much about the world were now opening the skies and allowing a downpour to fall upon everything I had not yet accepted about myself. I thought I had summed up Ebonia. But on this dark, yet enlightening day, I quickly learned that Ebonia had summed me up, as well.

That's the bitter price of delusion, I guess. Surely, a race, or a person, no less, can look within, take stock and decide if it is better to be someone else or something else. Sometimes the answers to life's mysteries can be pieced together from the stories people tell, from how their days have molded their lives, as well as how their lives have shaped their days. Some have so much to say, while others say so much in only a few words. For three beautiful years, the rapture and pain of this little town had captivated me.

At The Chinaberry Tree Bar, however, Ebonia's eerie dichotomy was fulfilled and yet vanished into thin air. Men, and a few faithful women, entered its doors six days a week for the latest, along with traditional drinks and provoking discourse. Above a long mirror that extended from the front of the bar all the way to the end of it was a small placard with the words, "Dedicated to Melvin Hart." It was in this long, narrow hallway of an establishment that I had received the equivalent of three Ph.D.'s. The conversations often were lively, crass, sometimes downright raunchy or unbelievably profound.

No library could hold the insights I gained from the brilliant yet grassroots men and women who brought their lives with them to this hallowed ground of shot glasses, myriad fragrances and unbridled philosophy. These vibrant and tired lives were emptied on the tile floors of The Chinaberry Tree. An imperialistic anthropologist, I would siphon their experiences like an addict snorting cocaine, hopelessly transactional. I watched in amazement as, on some days, someone would pick up a moment, hoist it over a shoulder, and carry it home as a replacement for a soul lost, only to have it evaporate before entering their doorways.

The men and women of The Chinaberry Tree represented the beauty and repugnance of the human spirit. They were both naïve and grounded; focused and misguided; and proud yet sad. My frequent visits to the bar had afforded me a chance to come to know many of them—some perhaps too well—outside the bar setting. While The Chinaberry Tree was open weekdays, I knew best the group of patrons who tended to frequent the bar on Friday evenings or throughout Saturday. Those were the primary times of my visits. Depending on my visit, I would see a different crew, although some would change their drinking routines on occasion. There were about two dozen or so main ones, but I had learned about them all. Each was on a unique journey to their own sacred shrine.

For instance, there was Brad, a tall, college-educated, opinionated black knight of sorts. He changed girlfriends like underwear, and most regulars at The Chinaberry Tree had given up on the possibility of ever getting a wedding invitation from him. Whenever he entered a room, people knew they were in for a speech. He had this penchant for weak women, but in a matter of days he would hate them for being so emotionally fragile. Nonetheless, women seemed to like confiding in him, and he often provided very good advice, although the price of the counseling often ultimately entailed their having to go to bed with him.

Enoch, on the other hand, was a likable five-foot, nine-inch man of average build and light brown complexion. Although a nice fellow, he was a hopeless underachiever. He countered this by countless forays about how life was a game already decided. He worked for the local retail store as a stock clerk and had been employed there for a number of years. While there was absolutely no opportunity for advancement, he did not seem to mind.

Then there was James. He was like a brother to me, and sometimes I'd call him that. A big mama's boy, he was compassionate, without being too soft. He headed the local senior citizens center and could incite an Old Fossils protest at the snap of a finger. An elderly family member, who died only recently, reared him. We talked about his inner feelings a lot here at Bo Willie's bar, especially during the days immediately following her funeral.

Even ancient ass Piper is staring at me now, and with a hint of pity. The oldest of The Chinaberry Tree gang, Piper, a retired theatre director and playwright, decided to make Ebonia his home. After all, his best friend had died, and now he was able to screw the deceased geezer's wife, when and if he could get it up. Sure, he has a pantry of experiences and "the heart of a young buck," but how dare he try to judge me!

Trent, tucked over in the corner, was a starving artist whose luck in New Orleans landed him atop—literally—an older, well-off woman. He anguished over her fatal illness, but she took care of him handsomely. Now established, he selected Ebonia as his quiet homebase to carry out his first love and to listen to jazz.

Ruth, Ruth. I *really* like Ruth. Single and independent, yet not quite as emotionally strong as she pretends to be. We have lunch together sometimes near the campus of the big state U over in Saxonville. Sadly, Ebonia sometimes had a way of making you see the world in simplified terms of black and white. There was Ebonia and the accepted, and the rest of the world. Ruth worked at a firm in Saxonville that was headed by a domineering black guy going through a midlife crisis. She hated him, but she loved the money. When she visited a favorite cousin in Ebonia on Friday evenings, she'd often stop by The Chinaberry Tree for a drink. Although she intimidated the shit out of a lot of the guys at The Chinaberry Tree, the two of us seemed to hit it off from the onset.

A Vietnam veteran, Bo Willie was perhaps the saddest and most interesting character of the whole Chinaberry Tree lot. He had the heaviest voice, which he turned up like an expensive concert amplifier whenever he wanted to make a point. He shared ownership of the bar, served as its bouncer in a heartbeat, and was often approached by the barflies with kid gloves. To many of us, he seemed invincible.

But then there were those few occasions when Bo Willie completely lost it. One such time was during a conversation at The Chinaberry Tree that centered around those things in the past that have led to black folks in America being so, as he put it, "fucked up" at times. Bo Willie unloaded his past like a machine gun of flashbacks, a Prufrock stranded in a Detroit titty bar. No one who happened to be in earshot that particular afternoon ever saw Bo Willie as the same person again.

The Very Wrong Reverend Wright worked with James at the Senior Citizen Center. Irreverent, but a lot of fun, the good pastor had some *serious* issues, especially when it came to his perception of women. A true shepherd he wasn't, but his charisma kept him afloat at work and among his flock.

David was a pretty nice fellow, too. He kept to himself and was the choir director at Ebonia College. He had a love for the Negro spiritual that was unsurpassed, and he had perfected its delivery using the Ebonia Spiritual Singers as his instrument. He worshiped the work of William Dawson, considered the father of the spiritual, and Dawson's influence was evident throughout his work. Because of David, Ebonia College boasted the most respected choral group among historically black colleges and universities.

Now, every town has its unofficial mental case. For Ebonia that was Crazy Hezekiah. As a once-sane high schooler, he helped Papa Schaumburg compile the town history, which the latter referred to as "a prologue to the Black Experience." Ebonians believe there was something in the old man's records, later lost by fire, that drove Hezekiah out of his mind.

Mr. Lewis was often the voice of reason at The Chinaberry Tree, unless, of course, Bo Willie or Brad were on a pure rampage. He had garnered quite a bit of property, along with a respect in Ebonia owing to his generosity. From a poor Alabama background, he had transformed himself into a major landowner. A retired superintendent, he had taught at several school systems in the Southeast and was known for his connections.

Ebonia College had a gifted archivist named Franklin. His forte was the documentation of the administration of former Ebonia College president, Hamilton Savery, whose past he had reconstructed through massive interviews held back in Mississippi and partially with assistance from Savery's old friends. Franklin usually quenched his thirst with gin and tonic on Saturday evenings.

Another regular was Peter, whose return visits to Ebonia had become more frequent. His father had been elected city councilman and lived in a newly developed neighborhood on the west side of town. A Chicago psychologist by trade, Peter was trying to move closer to home and even had placed a resume with Ebonia College's psychology department. His younger brother Paul was a down-to-earth guy working on his master's at Tuskegee.

Isaac Speights was no doubt the smartest man in Ebonia. The principal investigator behind several major higher ed STEM grants, Isaac could lead a discussion on a wide variety of topics. His pet peeves, though, were slow learners and lazy people.

Shit. *Shit*. Ray-Ray. He was a wannabe militant who passed around often-memorized statements from black historian John Henrik Clarke as though they were fried chicken. He preached that African Americans needed a well-crafted master plan in order to really excel throughout this century, but he never wrote *anything* down.

Pookie was the walking pessimist who never got over his childhood experiences. The end result was an embittered man who regarded life as something that simply had to be endured rather than lived and appreciated.

The forever-suave Tony had serious political aspirations, but ironically he was also saddled with irrepressible fears that someone would look into his closets to discover skeletons that could dramatically alter his life.

Most women left a bad taste in Tommy Lee's mouth. A borderline misogynist, he manipulated a bitter taste for women into his expansive ownership of several local businesses.

Tank was Ray-Ray's best friend and top cheerleader. He had become so accustomed to serving as backup to Ray-Ray that he failed to develop a mind of his own. Despite his black militant rhetoric, he harbored a weakness for white women of which not even Ray-Ray was aware.

Melvin Hart was a sickly dude who died about a year ago from sickle cell disease. He made quite an impact on people, though. The rumor had it that he was bartender Porter's illegitimate son.

Of all the people who frequented The Chinaberry Tree during the afternoons and evenings of my visits, the biggest set of balls belonged to an old woman named Ethel M. Mann. A lesbian of legendary proportions, she was another perfect example of how even the most Christian of towns can ignore the detestable, if it stands a better chance at benefiting through the association.

There is a fairy tale about a little boy who honestly exclaims that the king he sees parading on the street before him is naked. If Ebonia were a fairy tale, Sonny would be that boy, and Reverend Wright would hold the indubitable distinction of being His Royal Highness.

Finally, Joseph could be called Ebonia's Prodigal Son. He rarely visited the place of his birth. When he returned home, he did everything he could to remain detached from the community, so even many longtime residents knew nothing about him. He treated the hallowed Chinaberry Tree like the wayward stepchild he had become. He had thick, curly hair, and his voice was that of a traveler from a faraway place.

***

Never has there been such a range of pain and ecstasy, promise and futility, in so small a space. I know all of these people, these beautiful, strong and brutally hurt human beings. Because of their words and souls, I know I have an answer to Bo Willie's question. But it is buried deep inside me and has to be actively sought with the right probing.

Long ago, I had cast down my buckets among them, down in the filth and splendor of a modern and Chaucerian human essence. My eyes had never seen life as pure as I had found it in the dark, dark eyes of these African souls assembled in Alabama's Black Belt, where each weary heart seemed destined to balance a world upon the shoulders while going about a pilgrimage of unknown end.

These souls were the magical moments in time who gathered for the pilgrimage each week, seeking nourishment and shade at The Chinaberry Tree. They formed a world within a world that I had learned to savor like fine wine. They left an imprint in my mind, despite its endless stream of consciousness, and they were *my* people.

Chapter 2 – Brad's Tale

Simply mention male-female relationships, and Brad Fairheart would jump on his soapbox. The others in the bar would humor the young bachelor from time to time as his forays into the mind of James Joyce ran their course. But then there also were those times when they preferred just talking and instigating bullshit over listening to anything hovering anywhere near profundity.

Brad was the learned man who liked "talking about pussy" as much as any other guy. But as Bo Willie had so often noted: he couldn't seem to "get pussy to stay with him" for any significant amount of time. After he had his rum and coke and had departed, someone would hypothesize that Brad's problems came as a result of his "thinking too much."

"Too much thought can kill a brutha," Bo Willie once said, perhaps in a half-assed imitation of Cicero, spinning around on a barstool one Friday evening. The bar gang chimed in, "Amen."

There was no better evidence of this diagnosis than one late spring Saturday. Brad had entered the bar in a gray jogging outfit, a pair of white Adidas and a matching gray headband.

"What's up, my people!" greeted Brad, obviously in good spirits.

"You da man!" a few responded in an almost instant reenactment of the black church's Amen Corner. Enoch then looked up from an early morning Bloody Mary and asked Brad about his latest girlfriend. Uh-oh. It was show-time.

"She's gone," Brad answered abruptly. He motioned Mr. Porter to prepare him a drink like Enoch's. On cue, Mr. Porter went to work like an alcoholic's George Washington Carver. In his mixing glass, he poured a jigger of vodka, followed by a blood-thick tomato juice and a slight squeeze of lemon. He reached under the counter for Tabasco, a bottle of Worcestershire sauce, adding to the concoction alternate dashes of salt and pepper. He then stylishly added ice and shook the ingredients expertly before straining it over a single ice cube in an Old Fashioned glass.

"You know," began Brad, accepting the drink as though it were a coveted NAACP Image Award—Mr. Porter *loved* this about Brad—"hope makes it easy for men to overcommit themselves to the job, friends, family and personal relationships." He looked to his left and found an empty seat at the bar.

"We find ourselves working long hours, bailing a friend

out again 'for the last time,' trying to recreate a loved one, or holding on to a relationship that everyone else is expecting to disintegrate. Why?"

"What do you mean, 'gone'?" asked Bo Willie slyly, stirring the vodka in his own Anybody's Special.

"It's four-letter word, asshole," hissed Brad. He continued, answering his own question and sipping on his drink. "Why? Hope, I suspect. We men, too, are capable of housing it. For instance, we often pour our souls into our jobs, working thankless, nowhere positions that drain more out of us than we can ever hope to gain by way of money. We find ourselves driven by the notion—even if a mistaken one—that our efforts are 'needed here' and that the workplace will fall apart at the seams were we to leave."

"One monkey don't stop no show," commented Mr. Butler, cracking his bartender's towel like a whip. Pieces of lint danced from his shoulder to his waist and then formed a miniature whirlwind on the black and white tile floor. Then: "What are you having?"

Trent, The Chinaberry Tree's artist-in-residence, liked testing the bartenders' skills by ordering what he believed to be more complicated drinks. "How about a White Russian?"

"Coming up," said Mr. Butler.

"You're right," acknowledged Brad. "One monkey *doesn't* stop the show. But perhaps we men need this feeling as much as we need blood. You know the feeling: indispensability. It's a feeling we don't always experience at home, because home is often the term's antonym and where our sense of insignificance incubates. While we may come home with tales of being the supermarket's best bagger, McDonald's most efficient night manager, or the best janitor in the bank's history, we are hurting inside because we know that our job—our place in the world—is but a piece of something much greater. We work, sweat and perfect our mediocrity in hopes that things will become more significant along the way."

"The object is to simply play the game," suggested Enoch. "Friends, family and jobs are all props of the game. There is no winning. You just have to play the damn game."

Mr. Butler, perturbed, seemed to be having trouble locating his coffee brandy. He liked order and system. He was to alcohol what Brad was to pompous discourse. In his mind, if Ebonia was a Sodom that could only be saved by him, it would be his scientific precision and lengthy drink repertoire that would keep the little shit-ass town from going up in flames. Now possessed, he checked several parts of the shelves underneath the entire length of the bar before discovering the special brandy under the section of the bar right beneath where Trent was sitting.

Now back at his station and in his element, Mr. Butler poured his vodka, along with the coffee brandy and a little milk he pulled from a small refrigerator placed beneath a large shelf on which the cash register was situated. He poured the mixture in an Old Fashioned glass and stirred and sanctioned it before eventually handing it to Trent.

"I've been guilty of allowing friends to occupy too much of my life," continued Brad. "Usually, somewhere in the middle of a task for one of them, I'd find myself saying, *I can't believe I'm actually sitting here doing this.*

"Don't get me wrong: friends are a Godsend," Brad went on. "But even the best friends will trample on your good nature like kids on an ant bed. They'll sometimes ask favors that they *know* will put a severe strain on your time, your loved ones or even your resources."

"'Have to say, 'fuck 'em' sometimes," humphed Mr. Butler as Trent and others nodded in audible agreement.

"Be that as it may," started Brad, "yet we men—"

"Turkey, say *some* men!" shouted Bo Willie. "You can't speak for *all* men. All the other bruthas in here have secure pussy at home."

"Damn." Brad tilted his head to search the floor, in disgust, as if wondering who had let out this Mr. Magoo-like chimp that had the audacity to pose as an insolent black man. "Alright—*some* men have a tendency to perpetuate this loyalty to manipulative friends. Let me use Bo Willie as an example, since he's dying to be seen and heard."'

Brad stood up for a moment and walked eastward toward an old jukebox in a pseudo-solemn manner, as though he was about to make his third bow in Mecca. But rather than walk completely to the jukebox, he quickly turned around, drink held gentlemanly in hand, and continued his point, like a salesman who had just been told *no*.

"Bo Willie, for instance," he continued, slowly framing his words as though his college tenure depended upon them, "could be a smelly, dumbass, low-down dirty baboon. And, everyone, from Ebonia to Timbuktu, can plainly see the mold and penicillin dripping from his ancient ass but me."

"Go on," coaxed Enoch, begging for the ultimate point.

"I'm saying," continued Brad, "I could go on forever trying to be this worthless piece of shit's savior, but nothing will get better. For what does it profit a man to waste a divine intervention on an orangutan? I mean, it would never dawn upon me to stop, look back and assess the situation."

There were a few chuckles among the men, an unbridled laugh from Mr. Butler, and a look on Bo Willie's face that suggested he was still waiting on the moral of the story. The insults had slipped away from him like a whore on cheap sheets.

"I believe that when I keep giving and giving to the likes of a Bo Willie, it's got to be much deeper than my simply liking Bo Willie. Anyone see what I'm saying?"

"Yeah, you're saying you's a faggot," added Bo Willie anxiously. "I ain't mad at you, dog. Who could resist all dis?" He then tugged on his crotch. "But den again, you could be a smart-ass Ken Nort'n, just waitin' on a beat down from an Ernie Shavers."

Brad found himself being forced to quickly make a point in the middle of the thunderous laughter and knee slapping of traitors.

"Well, what d'ya know," he commented, getting exasperated, "who said, 'you can't make a jackass drink?' What I'm driving at is that by trying to fill the bottomless pit evident in certain friendships and relationships, perhaps we are *really* trying to convince ourselves that we are worthy of love and caring."

Bo Willie, for the first time that night, sat in sonic silence. The glasses rattling behind the bar sounded like delicate piano keys, stroked by Teddy Wilson, with wayward, teasing fingers, sometimes straying away from the keyboard and getting stuck in the groove of a soft, brown spine.

"I mean ... it's not about the person we are helping, at all," said Brad. "We keep giving, we keep believing, we keep sacrificing, because the person has become a symbol of us. We want love, we want care, we want meaning. But, at the same time, we think that we are unlovable, hopeless and futureless ...

"Hope," Brad began to wrap it up. "It can be a frustrating possession. Just as many women want to change us—like that girlfriend who is no more—we, too, desire to change them. We brothers must force ourselves to remember those beautiful qualities that drew us to the mystique of our respective women. We can't afford to chase after the pieces of the perfect woman that we find represented in different women—a pair of breasts here, a nice, plump booty there."

"Nothing wrong with the power of the booty," added Mr. Butler. He likely hadn't heard shit else, just the word *booty*.

"Nor the tit," added Trent, to no one's surprise. He was often that person that put a tail on something that did not need a damn tail. He quickly went back to sketching on his pad. Anyone near him saw an impressive drawing of a stunningly beautiful, classy and exotic African American woman, with very nice breasts.

"Maybe so," Brad commented, "but by viewing a woman

as the sum of her parts, we unfairly depreciate the whole woman, humiliate her—not because of how she perceives herself, but because of what our limitations force her to become."

"But women play games, too," offered Enoch. "They accentuate their parts as assets."

"True. Maybe it's reciprocal," reflected Brad. "But if there's a perfect woman, then we must be willing to be perfect men, because perfection demands the best. I believe many men are engaged in a fruitless search for the perfect woman, one as perfect as she is elusive. These guys, too, are prisoners of hope.

"Men are fighters, we are taught," Brad continued. "It's noble to persist, exhibit loyalty and to demand that your women represent the personae of the novel in your head. There'll always be some blue-eyed hero to save the world at the climax of the movie or when the novel ends. Everyone else—simply hit the lights on the way out. That's purely American crap. As long as you limit your scope to another man's worldview, you'll never be heroic."

"I was following you," commented bartender Porter, pulling himself a stool, while Mr. Butler began wiping glasses and the countertop. "But then you lost me with the worldview."

"Sometimes we hold on to the wrong things," offered Brad. "How about a parable?"

"Go for it," said Porter.

"Suppose a man rolled a covered wagon up to you with bread, meat and condiments and told you that if you bought a sandwich from him, you would never be hungry again. You sacrifice a few immediate pleasures to buy the sandwich. You tear into the sandwich and, sure enough, it is delicious and filling. But then the man who sold the sandwich to you packs up his wagon, tells you he's going to get something to eat, and begins to roll on. Why not fix *yourself* a sandwich? you ask. He tells you that the sandwiches aren't for him or that he is allergic to the bread or the meat ... some bullshit. Then three or four hours later, you realize that you are hungry again but don't have any more money.

"Now just swap a few things around," gestured Brad, before sipping his drink. "The salesman is the white man. You represent the people of color all over the world. The miracle sandwich is a recreated Christianity, Islam or whatever pervasive doctrine that actually came out of your own cupboard. The money is your future."

"You're saying we've been sold a sandwich?" asked Enoch.

"A man who *knows* his future is secure doesn't need a fucking sandwich! In order to steal your future from you, you have been sold a religion without calories. You'll get your blessing in the next life. But in the meantime, the sellers are getting theirs now, all while peddling to the masses sandwiches that have no substance. So if the sandwich is just a temporary relief from hunger, then maybe the religion just holds you for the time being, as your son is emasculated, your wife, daughter and sister are raped, and that thing that is your African birthright is pulled right from under you."

"No more drinks for you," laughed Mr. Butler. "How'd

you get from talking about perfect booty to holy sandwiches?"

"Hell if I know," answered Brad, laughing at himself, then grasping: "I guess I'm saying that this span of history has gone on for too long. We black men, the people of the earth, made from soil in our black God's image, have been fighting for far too long. Something's gotta change.

"Black men must never lose hope in themselves nor their fellow brothers and sisters," said a now somber Brad. "We can't lose sight of what is necessary to return this world to a path of success. Our black women, in all of their wisdom and splendor, must find ways to keep us focused on that success, while keeping any doubts about our leadership to themselves. It's a tough task, 'cause sisters like to be in control. But I have hope. There's still hope."

Chapter 3 – Enoch's Tale

I first met Enoch at a worn-out retail store that had long outlived its prime and was gradually beginning to take the neighborhood down with it. He walked with a bounce and an air of authority, hauling a large, almost Ethiopian-shaped head along with him as he went through the store's aisles finding cheap bullshit for senior citizens. If you didn't know him, you would have sworn he probably owned a slew of these rundown five and tens.

Although a nice fellow, he was a hopeless underachiever. And, as if he overheard the criticism, Enoch seemed to counter this by endless forays about how life was a game already decided. He worked for the local retail store as a stock clerk and had been employed there for a number of years. There existed something about his demeanor that would cause others to think that he owned the damn place.

While there was absolutely no opportunity for advancement, he couldn't care less.

In our private conversations, Enoch said he often dreamed of being a king, winning the ultimate victory and making the then "colored folks" of his austere boyhood feel good about themselves. In those dreams, which traversed decades back and forth, he was always well-liked, and neighborhood mothers smiled at him, just because he was a good kid.

But in his past reality, most of the mothers on Ebonia's west side of Tulow, hated the 12-year-old Enoch. Then, he was often the subject of their ship-bashing gossip and a reachable ram in the bush for their discontent with their own lives. And, while their own offspring could have been thieves and roughnecks, the women deep within their hearts of hearts thanked God for Enoch. Surely, no child could match the hell-bound, bike-stealing, mannish Enoch Norman.

No one had ever seen Enoch's father, for that matter. Even his mother had only met him once and through what, she jested jovially with a close friend, was a divine evening came Enoch, the name taken from a sermon by an interim preacher-lover. The fact of the situation was, if any on the west side would simply own up to it, no small number of the mothers there had seen their children's fathers in a while, either. However, Esther prided herself in not having to mask this truth behind church socials and Sunday amenities.

Moreover, she felt no shame in having had an illegitimate son. What the fuck did illegitimate mean, anyway? Were the babies that mangy-assed white men had by black women on the plantation illegitimate? Of course not. When the law is a bastard, illegitimacy is its father. But, to the neighboring mothers' discontent, Esther made no secret of her inner desires as a woman, especially to her outcast gay friend, Head, who worshiped her words and movements like a limp eunuch charged with some seedy ghetto harem. Being a mother in no way relieved her of what she deemed as her right to sexual fulfillment. The other mothers, being the Sanhedrin Council that they were, found her utterly disgusting.

And, don't even mention the older church-going biddies and their husbands! The very idea that she would carry herself so loosely and allow that flamboyant sissy in and out of her house. If Esther had been in another decade, she probably would have been praised for being ahead of her time, being ultra-liberal or simply seeing people as they were. But, time is a bastard, too, and people are placed where they are placed in the cosmos. And, even though that's jacked up, people should at least be afforded some consideration for the utter fuckery of the time they are placed in.

Still, the women's utter contempt by sheer osmosis permeated their children, themselves—as Enoch—hopelessly lower class but—unlike Enoch—without knowledge of the fact. The children in the neighborhood became cold and indifferent whenever he would come around them. These often-feigned actions delivered to them the delusion that they were, somehow, in spite of a truth clear only to outsiders, higher up in the ghetto caste system.

With all the attention accorded him by the better lot of the poor, Enoch was forced to associate with those who, too, for no fault of their own, were riding on the ship with Jonah. These passengers included seasoned pickpockets and pickled drunks and losers who all lived void of dreams in the quarters among the stench of chitterlings, ancient shepherds and contemporary musk, with no one to walk along the alley to preach against their sins. The quarters within this parallel Nineveh comprised that definite one-block square, that one apple which set off the chemical reaction that ruined the entire neighborhood.

Those Blacks who had been fortunate enough to educate themselves at the colored schools assigned to them had quickly occupied the homes on the other side of a six-foot concrete wall that separated the poor coloreds from the coloreds who thought they had a shot at the American dream. Any fool from one foot outside of the South could see that segregation was a glorified sham to make poor whites blind to the fact that they were an integral part of the wretched of the earth.

Indeed, Blacks *had* to form the foundation, because without them the entire bullshit system would collapse. Mr. Giovanni, Mr. Murphy, Mr. Stein, Mr. Singh—none of them—could so timely merge into the sea of whiteness without there being a group to despise in unison.

For Enoch, the stink of this reality became a symbol of home and a form of mental freedom. There, on the flipside of the alleys of the quarters, lived a world of equals within a photographic negative. As filthy, ugly and vile as they were, those inside the quarters were united by the very things that kept them apart from on one day yet linked to the greater neighborhood on another.

Inside this picture negative of Babylon was a world not concerned about President Johnson's easing of the bombing in North Vietnam. This world knew of Adam Clayton Powell but relatively little *about* him. It knew word-for-word the songs of Glen Campbell and Dionne Warwick, but it did not know where Phoenix was nor how to get to San Jose. About the only word uttered and understood by all was "King."

Martin Luther King, Jr., substituted as a father image for young Enoch. Although he had never met the man, King and "the dream" would become the most important things in the entire black world. The essence of his royal charisma had even swept into this tiny village within the hamlet of Tulow.

Every day Enoch would ride through this microscopic world, and every day he would leave it to see other, cleaner, richer, whiter worlds. Just blocks away was the Country Club, where several mothers from his world worked. The homes were beautiful, representing several different architectural styles. The lawns were always impeccably green and the white 12-year-olds rode minibikes instead of dilapidated bicycles.

Enoch told me that sometimes they called him "Nigger!" But sometimes, too, he found work in the Country Club, doing odd jobs. He remembered the white mothers and their smells of pleasing powder and perfume. Smells of success and otherworldliness. On occasion, they smiled when they paid him. For some people, and Enoch always seemed to be one of them, a little white patronization could go a long way. Because of the occasional smile, his psyche would become gassed up and life was good.

No one in this different and green and orderly world knew that his mother had bought, perhaps knowingly, a stolen bike, but everyone in it knew he was poor, he was black and what his options were. In the quarters, everyone knew the bike was stolen, perhaps taken from some child only slightly better off. Yet they also believed that having bologna and bread kept one out of poverty. Options were what only God provided, and sometimes they were handed out to blessed individuals and other times they were handed out by the generations.

It made sense, somehow, to Enoch. The God that allowed generations of suffering surely had to have generations of blessings in store. When Enoch first told me this as we were having a drink in The Chinaberry Tree one day, it entered my mind that there were two types of people in the world. One group that wants its blessings in the here and now, and the other that actually believes it will get its prizes in the next life. Know that and you'll never have to know shit else.

Nonetheless, when pressed, people, even the residents of the quarters, would reason that a smattering of pleasures are deserved, simply for playing the game called civilized society. Thus, stolen pleasures were sometimes the only ones they could afford. Because their view of poverty was so tied to the material, they often missed what they lacked in terms of the mental and the spiritual. Because they were so trapped in the square box of American exceptionalism, they could never know that true life, which meant living without dwelling on it, was forever just out of their reach. Only a mustard seed of consciousness would beckon the least of them to fight, to dream, to struggle, to assimilate, to wrestle that unyielding angel whose forte' was always a blow to the kidneys.

Often, Enoch wrestled with the wayward angels who descended upon west Tulow in the form of poor mothers with Vaseline legs and who always refused his assistance through coarse and haughty tones. Yet sometimes, he said, their daughters would feed him moon pies in the backyard on certain spring nights, nights that were suspended by distant fried chicken or pork chops, burnt hair or the funk of someone's granddaddy. He would often leave those pigtails in the foreground of a darkening sky, amid the waning echoes of faraway peacocks, and would ride up the hill toward home, up, up where the dirt road seemed to meet the heavens.

After returning home from school one Thursday afternoon in early April, Enoch jumped on his bike and rode to the quarters, where he found the remainder of six boys forming a bicycle posse after one's father refused to allow him to join the group. "Where y'all goin'?" Enoch asked as he braked to a stop just in their midst.

"We gonna ride inda Country Club," said Tommy Lee, known among the quarters' bike riders for his eloquence and leadership abilities. If Tommy Lee said they were going to ride to the Country Club, then it was 'Look out, white folks, we gone ride in yo' Country Club.' Earlier,

Tommy Lee had wanted to hear some music from Joseph's pocket radio, only the radio needed batteries. Little Joseph had agreed to purchase the batteries in return for being allowed to tag along with the guys he pretended were his older brothers. Because the cheapest batteries were sold at the five-and-ten downtown, the seven rode first to Woolworth's.

As soon as they had finally entered the pearly gates of the Country Club, Li'l Man said, "Hey, y'all: dat one dare's my house."

"I got da nex'un!" exclaimed Daniel, also bitten by the bug of wishful thinking.

Beyond the bend, just beyond a Mediterranean-style house with a stucco finish and several arches, the seven heard the lawnmower sounds of minibikes and knew they would find well-off white boys speeding down through the valley. What they actually saw was a combination of minibikes and go-carts. One rider drove up the hill in a manifestation more of opulence than destination. He turned to the right, made a circle in the cul-de-sac, and came to a pause beside them.

"You guys wanna run?" the towheaded boy asked. He was riding in what looked like a real go-cart, not one that was pieced together from scraps of wood by some kid's enterprising father. Towhead was driving a Hawk fun-kart with what looked like a ram bar for steering with a pole shaft and assembly. A bent piece of metal affixed to the side of the cart served to hold into place the handlebar and allowed the entry of the rider's legs. There was a small flat vinyl seat with hardly any cushioning that almost mirrored the pad placed for the rider's back. Right behind the pad was a modified two-cycle lawn mower engine with the power to thrust the cart forward over 20 miles per hour. The tires in the rear were only slightly larger than the front ones.

The seven looked at each other, then toward Tommy Lee for a reaffirmation of their refusal to engage in a race out of their class.

"Naw," Tommy Lee replied. "We only got bikes. We can't run 'gins y'all."

The towheaded boy's friends began to ride up the hill toward him, sensing possible amusement.

"How 'bout just racing me?" said towhead. "I'll take on all of you." Again, Tommy Lee declined the offer and started to pedal on down through the valley.

"Tell me," addressed the boy to Tommy Lee's back, pissed at having been declined by a black boy having what seemed to be an iota of pride, "how much gas does it take for those things?" His friends laughed.

"I'll run 'gins you," said Enoch in a surprise utterance that broke up their amusement and awakened the six from the quarters.

"Are you sure you wanna try that?" queried towhead.

"Forget him!" Tommy Lee hollered at Enoch. "You can't win 'gins a go-cart! You crazy?"

"Dey ain't so fast," Enoch said, suddenly an expert on go-carts. "Where ya wanna race from?"

"Whoa!" said a blond boy on a minibike. "Uh-oh. That colored boy's ready to get beaten."

"He sho nuff is," added doubting Tommy Lee. "He's

gonna lose his head." The remaining poorhouse five agreed in unison. "Anyways, it's getting dark!"

"Let's race from down the road a piece," offered the towheaded boy, delighted to have a chance at the humiliation of outsiders. "We'll race down through the valley, and the finish line will be the oak tree at the top of the next hill."

"I'll give the signal," said the blonde.

The quarters' boys decided to rest on a slight embankment on the side of the road. Tommy Lee grabbed Joseph's radio and then took the bag of batteries.

"It's 5:45, and here's Simon and Garfunkel," said the Tulow DJ.

"He crazy," Tommy Lee told the others as he joined them on the grass to watch the massacre.

"On the mark," the blonde cried out. "Get ready ... Get set. Go!"

The white-framed go-cart jolted off down the hill, leaving behind a trail of faint blue smoke. The roar and tat-tat-tat of the motor echoed through the hills and pines. Enoch's right foot found the pedal of a bike too huge for him. It wasn't too unlike Jessie, the biology teacher's daughter, who had come on to him because she thought he was cute and took him in her backyard. She was older by at least three or four years. Her breasts were plump as cantaloupes but soft and yellow and with large nipples that unnerved him at first. She opened wide for him, and he pretended to know how their moment should end. Just like now. He entered her and heaven at the same time, never to return, withdrawing into cool hell air and thrusting into the fire of a heaven that damn-near short-circuited his brain. With all his might and weight he forced down the right pedal, then shifted his entire self, soul and all, to the left pedal, causing the bike to move to a slow but sure pace downhill.

The towheaded boy already was just ahead of him, and the vapors from the go-cart entered Enoch's nostrils and were as foul as Tommy Lee's vote of no confidence. Spinning a rock from its rear right tire, the go-cart swerved in front of Enoch's path, like Jessie did when he was innocently on his way home that day, but his bike was beginning to gain momentum as his buttocks swayed side-to-side across the long metal bar.

"Don't cum yet," Jessie had whispered in his ear, unaware that his rhythmic torment was keeping steady beat with this new unknown pleasure. He did not know what she meant. "You big for a little boy."

They both were tire-to-tire at the bottom of the valley and slowly, ever so slowly, Enoch began to climb the hill before them, climbing higher and higher with each sideward shift of his body upon the alternating pedals. He became one with the red, white and blue bicycle, and together they climbed the hill toward heaven and a dream.

"Go, Enoch, Go!" Joseph shouted in his jacket of many colors. And though the fierce roar of the go-cart nearly deafened him, Enoch heard the cheering of the guys from the quarters. They were with him. He must win it for them. He would be a king in the neighborhood.

The go-cart began to jerk and jolt up the hill. The towheaded boy began to curse and muttered what Enoch thought was, "Can't let a nigger win this race." But Enoch's steady strokes, the constant diet of bologna and white bread, coupled with the strong desire for a victory, took possession of the bicycle and, in the most difficult point of the hill, used Enoch as if to make some obscure point, sword in hand.

This hill, too, angled toward the sky, a blue dreamland, but Enoch's eyes were focused toward the oak tree that seemed to expand before him in a zany attempt to meet him. He began to forget about the towheaded boy and only concentrated on the solid oak. Within seconds he had passed the oak, then he turned around slowly and began to coast back down the hill toward the challenging go-cart.

"You're still a nigger," the boy said. Enoch somehow knew that the sneer was about something much bigger than him. If he was a nigger, then so was Martin Luther King. So were all the colored women working in the kitchens of the homes around the Country Club. The men driving the transfer trucks? Niggers. The ones building the house and roads? Niggers. But surely not Nat King Cole, Sammy Davis Jr. and Harry Belafonte? Yup: all niggers.

Enoch pretended not to hear him. After all, he had won. Hadn't Jessie ignored him that next day? Even after all the moaning and closeness and wetness? He dared to enjoy the breeze that cooled him as he sailed through the valley. It wouldn't betray. It pulled him in its bosom and lured him away from the earth. He had won, and he looked forward to the praise his friends certainly held in store for him at the top of the hill. His legs ached. His back hurt.

The inner sides of his thighs were sore from the constant friction and banging of the metal bar. He climbed what he hoped would be his last hill of the evening and found a brotherless Joseph waiting, alone.

"What happened to da rest of 'em?"

"That was great!" beamed Joseph, his jacket vivid and swinging about his frame. "You showed him."

"'kay," Enoch panted. "What about the rest of 'em?"

"Dey left."

"But how come?"

"Dey heard on my radio that King was shot."

"Dog!" Enoch said in disbelief, feeling a shadow of death.

"Yep," replied Joseph as they slowly rode back to the quarters, where Enoch escorted Joseph home. As he rode to his own home, he could hear folks talking about how good men always die, especially anyone trying to help colored folks. He heard men at the corner store saying that King should have left that Vietnam talk alone: Asking to 'take it easy' on niggers is one thing, they said, but white folks don't want you messin' with their war money. 'If a white man is making a dollar, it's 'ginst God and nature to buck it. Dat's the world we live in.'

When Enoch reached his house, he leaned the bike against the porch, walked inside the unlocked door, and fixed himself a bologna sandwich. He thumbed through one of his mother's used women's magazines. He rolled over on his back and looked at the dull, sagging and water-stained ceiling. Lately, Jessie had been acting more and more like a grown-up and was pretending she wanted nothing to do with him. Even his win in the valley in the Country Club was slowly becoming increasingly insignificant.

Within minutes he was taken by sleep, a deep black and dreamful sleep. In this darkness, color never mattered. People were the same, or so it appeared. It was a peaceful world that he loved visiting. There was no hatred simply because of differences.

When he woke up, Enoch told me that he realized that there wasn't a king in either world. Perhaps he was still a nigger in both, too. Finally, through his dreams, he later realized that the white mothers really had not been smiling at him; they were actually smirking. Maybe Tommy Lee was right: you can't win against the odds. There was no ultimate victory, just a new level of trials. Void of the most remote possibility of triumph, why even play the game?

Chapter 4 – James' Tale

Everyone at The Chinaberry Tree knows that James is like a brother to me. We have frequent conversations over drinks about his work at the senior center, his childhood and any other subject that happens to come up. He is the one who convinced me to put my leather journal aside sometimes when I talked with people around Ebonia.

"It could freak some people out," he had said. "People open up some, and there you are—a suspicious white guy—just scribbling away, like, like you are about to dash and place their lives on the evening news."

Then, he, point-blank, asked me what I was *actually* writing about. What kind of story was I hoping to tell? And, there was a pinch of sarcasm in how he used the word *hoping*. Usually, an empty compliment or a lie about my compiling a book of inspirational meditations would work. Sometimes, it took a combination of both. I quickly excused myself from my bro.

On this day, Porter had made me a simple rum and Coke. To appease James, I ordered one of Porter's specialties. He then took out a mixing glass, added some ice, about two ounces of whiskey, what seemed like an ounce of some type of syrup, a dash of orange bitters, and more aromatic bitters. After a quick stir, he expertly strained the concoction into a glass of new ice and handed me the Old Fashioned. I then joined James at the large window at the south end of the bar. The old, familiar group of The Chinaberry Tree had not yet started filtering in.

One of James' favorite seniors had died recently, and he was still a little down about it. He was wearing a long-sleeved black, white and gray block-stripe polo shirt. The shirt was form-fitting, but it was undermined by a flimsy collar that seemed to collapse around his neck, where the very slightest hint of a Dowager's hump was emerging. The tail of the shirt was folded under and rested atop a pair of near-pleated light-gray polyester pants that were cuffed and rode proudly above an immaculate pair of Stacy Adams.

"Someone told me not to be surprised if someday, without warning, I find myself crying uncontrollably, violently," James began, this time without the niceties of small talk. "That was a week or so after Momma died, and I had wearied of the half-assed sympathies. Sympathy then, I felt, was unwelcome and much too late. No one sympathized with me when I mopped wherever she had emptied her bladder on the hardwood floor, when she would struggle to keep sweets she should not have in her possession, when it took me hours to dress her for a doctor's appointment or to coax her to take a bath. So why should anyone offer me sympathy now?

"The last year of Momma's existence was the most difficult year of my life," James confided in me one night at Bo Willie's bar. "There were adjustments to be made, arguments to be heard, and painful diplomacy to be uttered in the wee hours of the night that constantly wreaked havoc on my ulcerous stomach. She was stubborn and ornery and often downright cruel, but she was my Momma.

"Momma was fifty-six when she accepted me from my real sixteen-year-old mother, who was incapable of taking care of me—or so the story handed down over the years had it. But even though—now that I look back—I can say she did one helluva job, given what she had to work with, there was a glitch. As a boy, I felt her need to prove she had 'the right stuff' as a mother for the first time, in spite of the fact that she was fast approaching retirement age, made her overly strict.

"There was no end to the teasing I put up with as kid for having to come in before sunset, or for not being allowed to go beyond the block. My captivity, as it were, became the subject of those who would call themselves my friends as well as those who could not stand my guts.

"'Someday, you'll thank me,'" Momma would say to me after denying my request to go down the alley to play with a buddy who was anxiously waiting. It was a wasted statement—as most statements are that are made by the parents of adolescents. You know: children live for the day. There is no concept of that vague someday. Sometimes it takes years before the notion becomes as clear as crystal. Usually, it is only when the kid has hair that becomes speckled with gray.

"But until that time, kids continue to live selfishly and to be cruel. I guess that's not really surprising, especially when taking into account how lowdown, insensitive and ignorant their parents can be. Since a much older parent raised me, my dress and personality were both subject to an older person's taste. I was taught to say, 'Yes, ma'am' and 'Yes, sir' in the presence of elders, and older people loved the hell out of it. Unfortunately, their children did not and hated the idea of being 'showed up' in front of their folks. Many told me that they were sick of their mothers comparing them to me.

"While my adolescent years were difficult, I did learn to admire Momma for her independence. For her, there was really no such thing as a man's job. She would mow the lawn, take out the trash, and massacre wasp nests and the like. But more importantly, she taught me that there was no such thing as 'woman's work,' either. Old ladies in the neighborhood praised me for being an impeccable housekeeper, but Momma's only regret was that she did not have a chance to teach me how to cook in case my wife got sick."

James had been talking a while, and there didn't seem to be a pause in sight. I was getting thirsty again, and I saw this juncture as a perfect time to come up for air.

"How about another drink?" I asked.

"Sure," he said, still looking out the window. "This time, Arnold, it's on me." He reached in his wallet and fished out some bills and handed them to me.

"No problem," I said. "Another Old Fashioned?"

"Absolutely."

Again, Porter was on point. In just minutes, I was returning to the table.

"Where did we leave off?" I asked, pushing the Old Fashioned close to his left wrist, which donned a Jaeger-LeCoultre Polaris watch with a mechanical alarm capability, a gift from the daughter of a long-ago deceased client.

"After her husband died when I was ten, we spent the next eight years together as mother and son, each of us being one-half of the other's life," James continued, almost on cue. "She prayed to the Lord to live long enough to see me finish high school.

"When I was in high school, Momma prayed to the Lord to live long enough to see me finish college. The Lord made her strong. She survived a stroke that, for a long while, left her with a limp. She often successfully combated diabetes and kept it tamed.

"In the entire eighteen years of my life, I had never seen her cry, not until one sunny Sunday in mid-August many years ago. A church member had volunteered to drive me off to college. As I looked through the side mirror, and then over mounds of bags and other belongings piled on the back seat of the old Buick, as we slowly pulled down the dirt road, I watched—mesmerized and numb—as tears streamed down her cheeks. I wanted to cry, because I felt a long chapter in my life closing. I just kept looking back, watching her stand in one spot on the porch, very still, tears flowing like the distant Nile.

"What a moving, unnerving sight. I guess I had always thought of her as two sexes rolled together in one: her strength was so formidable. Perhaps with this bitter chapter coming to a close, she, too, could grow again into the beautiful, more feminine woman that her love for me had denied her for several years.

"I cannot recall there having been tears when her brother James died in 1964, or when her husband died years later. What had been so significant about my going away to college—my worldly possessions tied up in plastic bags and cardboard boxes—that would cause her such anguish?

"That first year away, I wrote her and kept frequent contact with her. It wasn't long before I came to realize that my birthplace would never be a permanent home for me again. At college, I was learning a lot about myself and about black people.

"I learned, first of all, that the biggest backstabbers in the world are those who are still trying to prove something to themselves, and there were—and still are—many all over the world. I also learned never to assume that anyone has your best interest at heart. But most important of all, I learned to give respect and courtesies only when and where they were merited. Age alone, or position, was not any reason to hand out something as precious as respect. So, I resolved to have as little to do with any individual who could not regard me as an equal.

"There are things that one may never learn at home, and home does not have to refer only to a house with a family.

It can refer to a city as large as New York or a village like Tuskegee or Ebonia. In fact, it was in a mere village that I learned how beauties and beasts live together, reproduce and collaborate to control other people's lives.

"When I would come home on breaks from college, I would find that Momma's way of life was gradually changing. And it was changing at such an alarming rate that I knew it would probably be too late before I could offer her what she deserved. During the winters, she would confine herself to one room of the house. There she would bring any pots or plates of leftovers to place upon the space heater to warm.

"She was so plagued with dozens of nickel-and-dime insurance policies that offered laughable amounts at maturity that she had become a miser with lights, water and gas. Whenever I would visit, she would constantly tell me about the benefits all this insurance would provide me when she died. I rarely listened to her, and one day when she asked whether I wanted her to invest in my burial plot, I told her that I would be perfectly willing to let the people I leave behind to fend for themselves.

"'You're such a fool sometimes,'" she replied in contempt.

"But I thought the obsession with buying burial plots during one's short lifetime was the most absurd notion I'd ever heard. Old people's preoccupation with dying—at least the ones that lived in my neighborhood back then in Ebonia—tired me. If anyone, I reasoned, should be concerned about death and burial plots, it should be those pompous, over-fifty assholes on my job, the ones who were among the first to receive a college education but who had become totally ignorant when it came down to dealing with human need. It's easy to speak of loyalty, dedication and commitment when you're a balding, overweight and overpaid desk jockey playing with people's lives as if they were ants.

"Yes, elders' constant talk of death still gets under my skin," James continued, "but then there must be something to it. I mean, here you have people who have lived scores and scores of years. Here are people who have witnessed history repeat itself. So, what are they actually saying? I believe they are saying that it is time to expose 'life' for what it really is—a grand sham! From childhood we are taught to give freely for a payback that will come from another unverifiable source beyond this world. But, in reality, the purpose of existence is to ensure that you pay.

"Laws are made by lawyers and, ultimately, for lawyers. Mortgages are written to cover a person's entire working life. New cars are engineered to last as long as a payment coupon book. I believe old people have known this shit all along. Top the economic crap with being black, and there is no reason, outside of taking care of a child, to even bother getting up in the morning."

James took another sip of his Old Fashioned. His eyes were getting misty. He looked at the jukebox across the club in the far right corner. He stole a glance at Bo Willie, who immediately returned the glance with a smile and "the finger." James laughed lowly. He then looked at me as if he could see inside of me. I knew that I had only to sit quietly and continue to listen.

"Momma must have noticed over the years how tax forms and insurance policies were becoming increasingly complicated. She must have seen how her limited education was becoming taxed to the limit. She must have felt how un-American it was to not know how to drive. We welcome among us so many delusions under the guise of progress. Yet progress is juxtaposed with little old ladies in dimly lit rooms, meaningless programs that benefit only grant writers, and the growing bitterness of youth.

"This bitterness is kept in check only by the presence of a loved one who, in different ways, serves as a cushion between an individual and the harsh reality of the world. I guess you can say Momma was my cushion. Though I constantly read and learned and strived for the truth in and behind all things and people (perhaps the two are one and the same), the more I came to know, the more bitter I became. Yet my love for Momma was the central theme, and it, miraculously, outweighed what I perceived to be the stoic futility of life, of tomorrow.

"Throughout the years with Momma, I learned that there is no teacher among mankind, for we are all students. Life is the only teacher; death, the only degree. Every single day is a class; each forced smile, an examination.

"In that we all—no matter how great or gifted in philosophy—must die, it is almost laughable, right? I thought of all the arguments, the turmoil and strife of those years. But then I began to think of the last year I moved, and why it is that we erect monuments at all, or that we allow ownership to throw us in such frenzy. Like King Solomon, I sensed the futility. Yet when Momma died, I would have given every cent I had to erect a monument to her, to let all know how important she had been to my life.

"On a rainy Wednesday morning in March, I looked at Momma's still body in the upper room. The paramedics had come, found her dead and—as frequent contact with death would have it—asked if they could smoke in a side room while they awaited the coroner.

"'Go ahead,' I said, and I stayed in the upper room, staring at the one who had meant so much to me. The last year with her was difficult, yes; but it was also the best year I had ever shared with Momma. For one full year, I administered her insulin, prepared her meals, and constantly reminded her that I was not her dead brother, but her son. Throughout the entire year, I could not convince her. I simply answered.

"Still, her health seemed to steadily improve until another stroke just weeks before her death. Indeed, that is how my life has always been—a calm before the storm. Anyway, finally, the coroner came. I spoke with him in the hallway and answered yes-or-no questions. He looked at Momma and then placed his ear to her chest. The old gray man, who looked like he could have had a drink with death himself, proceeded to place his knee in her stomach and bore down with his full weight. A policeman made a cameo appearance and was off to another destination. Like Momma, I felt neither here nor there. I talked to the coroner in the living room, and for a short while I talked to no one.

"Then, the men came from the back room. And, they carried Momma in a plastic bag. Reality set in as they passed me in the hall. Like the mighty Nile oozing out of Ethiopia, I felt the essence of futility crashing upon me. I wondered about my purpose in this world, and I wondered about yours, too.

"What does it all mean, Arnold?" James finally asked me. "Of what merit is our struggle? Surely, the day will come when the prince and the bum, the Ph.D. and the imbecile alike, will be placed in plastic bags; when all their good or bad will be summed up by a vinyl and final judge. Speak then of tomorrow, if you can."

Then James looked at me in a way I had never seen formed by his face.

"Place this in that book you are dying to scribble in." His Old Fashioned was now down to a piece of ice about the size of a tumor on the soul. He tilted his head back and tossed forward the ice into the hell of his upcoming message to me.

"You know that small prayer chapel at Ebonia College?"

"Yeah," I replied. Everyone knew about that little chapel. Although Ebonia College was somehow affiliated with The Episcopal Church, which likely didn't mean a thing as support of its struggling black schools goes, the chapel was quaint, well-kept and revered. Its sanctity had never been compromised.

"I want you to do something."

"Sure. What?"

"You must go there with this burning desire of yours," said James, lowering his voice. "But not just at any time. Go there at a special time."

"Special time?" I asked, holding my hand over my glass and the 'What the fuck?' now inside it.

"Yes," he countered, looking toward Porter. "It should be something like the tenth day of the tenth month and the tenth hour. Something along that line. And, you should go inside that chapel with your thoughts. Just wait. Just listen."

"How will I know I'm receiving what I came for?"

"Stay until the reckoning," said James. "When you realize that you are a blue-eyed pawn, with no control over anything or anyone. You are as chosen as blades of grass underneath dog shit."

Chapter 5 – Piper's Tale

Older than some countries, yet as youthful in spirit and mind as a 30-year-old, the late Piper Lawrence liked to lure ears into yesteryear with tales about himself and his buddy, the late Langston Hughes. He was one of the first people I interacted with when I moved to the area, and he died within six months of our meeting. He suspended imaginations on a ride through much of his 90-plus years and left them with profound statements about the future of African-American drama. Piper Lawrence *always* had something to say.

Born in Greenville, Mississippi, around 1911, director Lawrence spent most of his early life in New Orleans and later graduated from high school in Kansas City in 1928. During his sophomore year, he ran for recording secretary of the Student Athletic Association. He claimed that a boy who would later court blues great Billie Holiday was his campaign manager. On the day of the campaign speech, though, the young man abandoned ship. He probably did the same thing to the jazz queen, too. Also while at Carver, Piper claimed he was taught music by a famous black conductor and choir director.

Long before launching his career as a director, Piper took bit parts in a few high school plays, among them "Kingdom of Heart's Content" and Channing Pollock's "The Fool." He then attended a Christian college out west, where he majored in English and drama. Soon disillusioned, he returned to Kansas City, organized a little theatre group after the Depression and married in 1934.

"I went back to Los Angeles in 1938," Piper told me once. "I met Langston Hughes through a mutual friend in 1939. I was anxious to meet him; he had written a poem that had created quite a stir. Some religious fanatics had even picketed his coming to L.A.

"I helped him organize the New Negro Theatre, and we later presented his play, 'Don't You Want to Be Free?'" Piper said.

After working with Hughes a few years and then settling in eastern Alabama, Piper said he was called to defend his country in the wake of World War II. Unabashedly interested in the occult, Piper visited a fortuneteller named Aunt Mary near Griffin, Georgia, to determine what the draft notice held in store for him.

Looking through her tea leaves, Aunt Mary chuckled. "I see they gotcha. But they ain't gonna keep you. I get six. Six days, six weeks ... but not longer than six months." She looked at her leaves again, and said to him: "I don't see a uniform on you."

His wife entered a music college in the Midwest, and Piper joined the U.S. Army in February of 1942 as an MP at a base in Texas. "During a serious drill, my leg gave way," said Piper. The incident brought to mind his bout with scarlet fever as a child, when he was forced to use a walking stick.

He went on sick leave, did his best as a soldier, but could not go on hikes. He was transferred to limited service as head of the Service Club. Soon, an order came through to release all limited service men with an honorable discharge. The order came on the day marking his sixth month of military duty, thus entitling him to full military benefits. When he returned to Alabama from the Army, he could hardly wait to drive over to Georgia to see Aunt Mary.

Piper later found work at a playhouse in California and landed a role in "Petrified Forest." Now with G.I. benefits, he went to acting school in 1944 at the Dramatic Workshop of the New School of Social Research, where his classmates included several budding stars.

"I returned to L. A. again in '47," recalled the director. He remembered once failing to land a job at MGM because they didn't want his lighter skin. The studio reasoned that it had several 'white' actors it could use in blackface; why use a Negro that had to be made up?

"Now, blacks are in a number of roles on- and off-Broadway and are on television," Piper commented, seemingly pleased. "There were so few roles for young blacks at that time. When there was a call for a black actor, several black asses would rush to meet it. But the parts usually required older, more mature players. It was a difficult profession to love. Even the well-off black families in Harlem and elsewhere were rarely supportive of those members who wished to pursue the acting field."

Piper recalled that Harlem was the true lifeblood of Langston Hughes, who lived on 127th Street among the people he loved to write about. "The last time I saw Langston was in the early '50s. I asked him about a parody skit he had written–*Limitations of Life,* I think–criticizing Fanny Hurst's popular novel–and he said he'd have to look in his files for it."

According to Piper, his friend Langston never obtained the financial position that would enable him to live well. He had to write constantly to make ends meet, and the poet's love of traveling consumed the little he had saved.

"I was in Jersey when I heard about his death," Piper said. "I always thought that Langston gave up and didn't fight for his life because of the accolades given the younger James Baldwin, who had received such ravings for *Go Tell It on the Mountain*. Langston had struggled so hard and had opened so many doors. This, of course, is my own opinion."

Piper also denounced books later written about the noted poet and playwright. "We are living in an age of dirt. It's a tell-all world, where everyone wants to know people's personal lives." As for his own life, Piper directed Hughes' "Black Nativity" in Oakland after finishing "Agnes of God" at a small black college in Alabama.

"Young black actors need to learn the craft and to take advantage of every opportunity to express it, whether that opportunity arises in a church, hall or theatre," he said, his voice wearying. "I would like to one day see a repertory touring drama company here that could be sent to Europe and China to show original black plays," Piper said.

"The future of black drama depends upon black writers, black producers and black money. Black financial backing is lacking to assist our black directors," commented the venerable. "Our writers are wonderful, but money is needed in all avenues. As it stands, the only encouragement a black playwright has is to hopefully get an agent interested in his work. Here, too, is an opportunity for a licensed, bona fide black agent."

A minute of conversation with Piper easily could become an hour, an enjoyable hour. Langston Hughes was but one of the many men and women who Piper claimed crossed his path. His love for drama was at once evident in his voice and was the theme of an extensive mental library. Although he's long gone, no doubt Piper will remain center stage in many hearts.

We later learned through that rare bar patron that, while serving a director's residency at a black college near Charleston decades ago, old-ass Piper had gotten a young international theatre student pregnant. The woman had a son, but no one knew his name nor the mother's, and they assumed she moved to London, where she had a Nigerian sister.

Chapter 6 – Trent's Tale

Trent had always heard about those poor souls who found themselves in positions, it seemed, that even the Man Upstairs chose not to intervene Himself. There were those times, he surmised, when people had to face the carnal reality of their most difficult problems without help from above. And when those Jobs had braved the storm, had been enveloped within the belly of the whale, they became strengthened in one sense, yet silently and decidedly less dependent on the One who 'allowed' the test. Reluctantly, Trent was warming up to me. God only knows what he saw when he looked at me across the bar table. If my count was correct, he was beginning his third Whiskey Sour, which was unlike him.

Just as I smelled a hint of lemon from his side of the table, so, too, did he sniff the faint hint of a friendly half-Italian who was blessed with a gift for gab. Then again, if he let his imagination soar a bit, perhaps I was like a blond, blue-eyed reporter who represented some leading art magazine. Mid-drink, however, I came to realize that his true difficulty, most incomparable in nature, had once rested naked on a bed beside Trent Fitzgerald. Partially disrobed, sweaty, sickly and determined, she had fanned herself with a few sheets of yellowed stationery and gazed at her lover-to-be through what she hoped were wanton eyes, yet through what she knew had to reveal some trace of the blues inside of her early fifty-year-old frame, the reds and browns within a shanty among the marshland.

The room, though peaceful yet far removed from the loud nature of the wild delta deep in bayou Louisiana, just miles away from the town of Venice, was filthy, almost too unclean to exist only an hour or so from the Cajun capital. Classical music from a once-abused radio found a corner of the room and was content to linger there. The room and the radio worked together to form a music box, an unlikely speck of heaven thrown somewhere off Highway 23, where it had dislodged into the twisted rust-colored bowels of land and water that engulfed the shack like a textbook cancer.

"If you'd just make it back to the highway," said Trent, sipping from his Whiskey Sour and staring out the window into the street, "you'd see otherworldly blue skies. Yep. An endless blue, but choked with huge cumulus clouds hanging so low you could almost piss on them!"

Whenever he'd stare into the distance, I knew he was thinking about her. And, from my previous notes, I also knew that the skies had darkened and he was out in the bayou again, overcome by his loins.

"Hasn't this become a part of our brief relationship together?" Mrs. Brittany had asked him.

"I never knew what to expect," he replied, trying to pull the music out of the corner it claimed. "From the time we first met in New Orleans, I have been trying *not* to expect anything at all."

Mrs. Brittany slowly, painfully, raised herself from the bed to fully remove her robe. "You are getting much too old to take life so lightly. It will pass you by. And you, too, will wonder why the young have lost their interest in you."

"But you're not well. You seem—"

"You seem like a young man who died a long time ago," Mrs. Brittany hissed, reminiscent of the lingering Mississippi that snaked around them less than a quarter mile away. "Perhaps you would have made someone a good doctor," the divorcee said, her eyes piercing the fidgeting nude body of the twenty-five-year-old sitting at the bed's edge. "Half the world is built on 'what seems.' The other half is built on 'what ifs.'"

She then took his hand and pulled him forward for a kiss, not unlike the time she had in the courtyard of Pat O'Brien's up in New Orleans. Only there they had sipped on Hurricanes and listened to the jazz, which slithered around the tables, and the visitors all pretended they had been to the tavern before. There, too, the skies had been a magical blue, and he could only see her through his youth and passion.

But that was a Mrs. Brittany that was before. That was before this remote stretch of the river had become nothing more than a breeding ground for hopelessness and despair. There are some things that simply aren't meant to be. Like roads that stretch lower than the river on their steady paths through hell, with sad cafes, stilted houses, stoic cemeteries and a few token palm trees sprinkled along them.

Before Mrs. Brittany, Trent had found contentment in painting portraits of visitors in Jackson Square. It was where he was meant to be. Free, set up within his arc of a large circle placed in the middle of a giant square. He could simply walk through the big wrought iron gates, pass the white horses and carriages, dash up thirty steps and be on the levee and within rock-throwing distance of that same damn Mississippi. On a good day, when he'd sold a painting or two, he might celebrate by dining at Dooky Chase on Orleans Avenue or Willie Mae's Scotch House a block over on St. Ann.

Before the tempting cougar had entered his life, Trent would sometimes spend an evening in his room in The Marigny neighborhood, making his own chalks, finding excitement and contentment in the endless possibility of colors. Some late weekend nights found him at Tipitina's on Napoleon.

And that was enough, albeit a slow painless death he had yet to realize. Until Mrs. Brittany, that is.

When she had sat before him for her portrait, he thought:

Here is a woman too beautiful to be left alone in New Orleans.

"Where are you from?" he asked as his pastels delicately teased the surface of his pre-primed canvas.

"Boston," she answered, striking a pose that aimed her gaze toward the old Jax brewery.

"You and your husband decided on a New Orleans spring, huh?" he probed.

"No," she replied, staring directly into his eyes. "The decision was all mine." The abrupt finality of her response offered an invitation to silence. The tone wasn't mean, and didn't carry with it a suggestion that he mind his own business. Some twenty feet away, visitors were dropping dollar bills in the hat of a teenage break dancer who performed a routine they could have seen back home for free—had they been willing, of course, to cross the railroad tracks that split their communities.

New Orleans, then, was an escapist's dream. And, in this lazy fantasy town he had bedded many an alcoholic, frustrated, married octoroon who had sought refuge from her own boring land of magnolias, ham hocks and upper-middle class semen, only to arrive in a world of her kind, prey to the young, darker, sturdier, earthier men she would have ignored in another Southern town.

But, somehow, Mrs. Brittany seemed different. She possessed an air about her that held the young artist and lover to her side, where he seemed happy to remain, if only for the present. She was not intimidated by the New Orleans heat and humidity. Her breezy, floral print sun dress with spaghetti straps accentuated large breasts which hovered over a shadowed waistline like a French Quarter balcony over Bourbon Street. Early one morning, a few days later, they would leave their motel room in Harvey and take her car back across the Mississippi into New Orleans.

It was in the Mecca of blues and jazz that Trent supported himself solely by his skills as a portrait artist. He was, in earnest, the child Billie Holiday used to sing about, the type of lover, perhaps, Esther Phillips would have slept with. He maintained the wit and politeness mothers of younger daughters loved, although he had been practically motherless himself. Moreover, he possessed a physique that made most men envious, even though he seldom exercised. Finally, he was to canvas what John Donne was to paper.

Mrs. Brittany at once saw these qualities in this handsome and talented, underachieving young man who, she honestly felt, was throwing his life away. She had watched him create striking portraits of visitors who sat before him and had vowed to meet him and to know him ... to be a part of him. Like magnets, their eyes kept meeting, pulling, as he dared to make woman from fabric of his canvas.

"I divorced my husband in Boston," she said a day or two later, almost as if someone had dropped a cue card she had been reading in the artist's eyes. Hours later, she was coaxing him into trying Escargot Bourguignon, Oysters Rockefeller and Chicken Rochambeau at Antoine's. The food was delicious, but he did not want to come across as a starving artist, so he tried as best as he could to control himself. Even Mrs. Brittany's appetite didn't seem to match her large request.

He balked, but after dinner, they walked along St. Louis Street all the way to Woldenberg Park, the hub for Steamboat Natchez. The street seemed to be the river-bound slit between New Orleans' old and new. They talked about life, but mostly about death. She said her ideal image of an exit from life would be to be left behind in such a way as to float aimlessly. At a point when their conversation had given voice to their footsteps upon the setts, likely as they crossed Decatur and North Peters, Mrs. Brittany asked: "Where do you live?"

"I have a room I rent from a little old lady on St. Claude Avenue," he replied, hoping to dissuade her. "It's not much, and it's on the other side of the French Quarter."

"Is she a busybody?"

"No. At least, I don't *think* so."

"Then let's go there." When she noticed in him a look of hesitation, she replied, "Hell, she'll think I'm your mother."

Truth be told, Mrs. Brittany was truly beautiful that night, an embodiment of a passion he had never before experienced throughout all his exploits and education of the princesses. The humid night seemed to last forever as the two lovers shared and traded youth and passion for passion and wisdom, as the tiny dark room began to spin and spin. And then, when it seemed as if both could endure no further dizziness, they were both lifted from the humble floor mattress by Lady Day, like babbling babes on a small stage along Bourbon Street, making songs within songs.

Why the hell then should we play throughout the day
We know it all leads to this same bed, I say?
'Cause no matter what love is, it's here
and here to stay.

Then, as they looked from the floor mattress through the lone window and into the night, out into the darkness teemed with souls, where the Mississippi had slipped into something more comfortable, they joined Lady Day on stage again for a private concert.

You, You, You
Don't know what I will do to you
You, You, You
Make these gray skies so blue-oo-oo

The voice, so intoxicatingly intertwined with feeling and life. If ever there was a cry for help, it escaped from the throat of Lady Day. A beautifully sad woman singing, singing, singing to a world replete with human imposters. The kind that posed with smiles and smirks before the twisted and burned bodies of lynched men.

We're in love?
Is this the utter test .. this song?
That melts the butter
Of your sweet tongue?
Come on, now, brother
Do - you - love - me?

How can you sing about love when you're dying? How long comes the restoration after the trials and tests of a hundred Jobs in succession? And, why didn't the thousands of ghosts drowned by surely extraterrestrial imposters cut down the flesh dangling from all the bridges over all the rivers? Lady Day's repertoire is suddenly less fruity. The air mattress slowly was becoming cold.

Can a heart beneath old breasts wonder
Of being loved above, and ravaged under?
Every hot sun sets, every wet kiss dries
Leaving it all to old tired eyes.

As days turned into weeks, Trent and Mrs. Brittany traveled the country together, each holding true to a silent agreement. He would never ask about the source of her seemingly endless supply of money, and she would never question his seemingly endless supply of time for her. When she began to get ill in San Francisco, it finally dawned upon him how little he knew about this older woman in his life. What was her background? What were her likes and dislikes? Why didn't she eat much?

He had intended to find out more in San Francisco after he left, at her insistence, their room on Columbus Avenue. When he returned from his pilgrimage through Portsmouth Square hours later, he found a note on the bed informing him that she had to go away for a few days. In the note, she pleaded with him to stay in San Francisco and told him where she had placed five thousand dollars for him. When he finally went to the desk clerk to pay the bill for their stay, the graying man informed him that Mrs. Brittany had paid in advance for two additional weeks of stay. During those days, he must have searched every street in the Bay area, especially around Fisherman's Wharf and

Bayview, and called every hospital. Finally, after he had been beaten by the cold winds, which offered no clemency when assaulting the cable cars, he decided to return to Columbus Avenue to face his last night at the hotel. As he opened the door, Mrs. Brittany, looking slightly swollen and puffy, smiled at him.

"'Been looking for me?"

That next morning, they packed all of their belongings into the trunk of her Cadillac and headed back to New Orleans. He worried if he would still have his room on St. Claude.

"Your mother paid for three months," said Mrs. Malveaux, beaming through brown, uneven teeth. Standing in the middle of luggage, he looked from the porch back to the car as Mrs. Brittany began to pull off.

"I'll come back later," she shouted and then coughed, a smirk pasted to her face.

When she returned for him that evening, she was a different person. Much of the gaiety was gone. For days she harped about his future, that he should do more, move to San Francisco or New York. She became less pleasurable to be around, even during their more private moments.

"You have a bright future ahead of you," she told him one day while they were finally driving south on Highway 23 again to Venice. New Orleans and civilization were only 77 miles away. They could have both been light years. "But you must be willing to meet it halfway," she continued. He had no idea what she meant, and she would never explain anyway.

To tell the truth, he hated this kind of talk. She was sounding far too much like a mother, and it was freaking him out. He would have lashed out, if only she didn't sometimes seem so much like a mother.

"The world has no respect for a struggling artist," she would always respond. "It would just as soon accept a no-talent rich man over a talented poor one."

His hands gripped the wheels with unanswered tension in the ten and two driving position. Was she about to tell him he was throwing his life away? Seriously? After pulling him away from his spot at Jackson Square to fuck him silly all the way to San Francisco and now back?

Their return ride to the marshy land in which Venice was situated was mostly a silent one. Maybe he needed to reassess his uncontrolled urges for these trouble-making, unattached older women. After they get the big dick that they been clamoring for, then they start looking for excuses to drop you to rein in their capsized emotions. As Trent drove down the lonely road, Mrs. Brittany looked out into the expansive swampland. He noticed her quiet gaze into the God-forsaken wasteland and thought: This bitch had better not try to leave me stranded in this damned shit land!

"I guess it's time," she almost whispered. He had almost missed her utterance.

"What was that?"

"Oh," she responded, as if stunned into the present. "I guess it's time to tell you how much you have meant to me."

"You don't have to tell me. I sense it." He was feeling a

little weird himself about now, travelling down this crazy road. In the weeks, she had caused him to think ... a lot. Before Mrs. Brittany, he enjoyed making the visiting cougars who wandered about New Orleans moan in ecstasy when he allowed them to pull him away from his post into their temporary bedrooms. "Take all of it," he'd whisper in their ears."

But, no matter how good he was or how good they were, they would leave and reclaim the lives back home.

"Sometimes, it's good to say it, nonetheless," she finally said. Highway 23 had gone as far as it could into the bowels of nothingness. To remove itself of any involvement for what could happen at this point and beyond, it approved the name change to Jump Basin Road. Then Jump Basin Road, realizing it had been duped, bailed out immediately at the bend and handed the remainder of the ride through hell to Tidewater Road.

"How do you feel?"

"A little tired." This was the end of what was sometimes called the Great River Road, a hodge-podge route that began in Minnesota and faithfully follows the Mississippi River through ten states, ending below Venice. Only, the road was the end "for most people." There were still options for those who chose to go just a little further, and Mrs. Brittany was one of those type of people.

"Why won't you tell me what's wrong? If you cared, you would at least try."

"Dammit, let's not go through it again! Please! I'm in no mood for this phony compassion! I have enough to contend with now without having to console a little boy!"

That was it. Trent pulled over to the side of the road. "So, is that all I have been to you? A boy, huh? A big dick? I'm a man when it comes to the physics of filling a hole, but a boy when it comes to trying to get a little respect! You're not all that complex, y'know. Let's sum it up: full of shit!"

"I didn't mean it the way it came out."

"Some things can't be taken back."

"Please. Let's make this a special trip," she said.

"Maybe I'll *never* understand you, Crystal," he sighed, starting the car again. "You seem like a sick woman, yet you want to gallivant around the country like, like a, a—"

"Young college girl?"

"No, that's not what I meant." That was *exactly* what he meant.

"Isn't it?" She placed a few strands of hair behind her right ear. "Never mind. This is a special trip, perhaps our last through Venice."

"*Last?* What do you mean?"

She didn't answer or say anything until they had reached Venice. There they met a mulatto named Jacques who drove them from the dirt intersection in an old Ford truck on another forsaken road. He parked and then secured to the truck a boat that seemed to be eagerly waiting to take someone somewhere down a canal and to a patch of an island, attached like a polyp in the bowels of the Delta.

He had driven them about three miles further south on a dirt road through a place where water and land were indistinguishable. He reached a spot to let them out. He then backed up a bit and unhitched the boat.

"Is everything okay?" she asked Jacques, who nodded

solemnly. Trent's imagination soared, but he said nothing. "Just in case you need these," said Jacques, handing each of them a pair of knee-high rubber boots. "Remember to turn at the three cypress trees." Trent hoped he was talking to Crystal. Jacques steered the Ford in the direction of the end of the road.

"Where'll we go now?" he asked, this time embarrassingly feeling like a little boy.

"Ever handle an outboard motor?" She attempted a smile.

"Never."

"I have," she said as she slowly, again painfully, climbed into the small boat. "Get in. Be careful now!"

The two of them slowly swerved through the tiny bayous of the Mississippi delta, watching the assorted wildlife either run or paddle to safety. He was terrified that they might be spotted by an alligator. She steered them past bayou cabins, fishermen's huts, and only occasionally did they hear over the motor the sound of a faraway hunter.

Finally, Mrs. Brittany aimed toward a little cabin she seemed to immediately recognize. When they had walked inside the decaying structure, Trent noticed a usable fireplace and a bed in fairly good condition, considering whatever means it must have taken to transport it to the shanty. "Close the door," said a solemn Crystal. "I need to talk with you. I need to let you know the truth."

"You don't have to tell me ... that you don't love me, I mean," countered Trent, guards up, always believing in a good defense. "I never expected love."

"No, Trent. That's *not* what I'm about to tell you."

She took his hand and made him sit beside her on the bed. "The fact is that I do love you."

"Is it about your sickness, then? Bad news?"

"To answer both questions: Yes and no." Somehow she managed a sincere smile.

"Well," Trent started in a sigh of relief, "that's news enough for me."

"Why don't we first take our own commercial and then come back for the rest of the news?" she coaxed. "Care to put your tail where it really shouldn't be?"

"I'm game if you are."

As he looked into her eyes, he once again saw the woman who had sat before him for a portrait months ago. Her skin was glistening from the penetrating delta sunset that sent a ray through a crack in the wall. Her seductive smile was an elixir that cured the disease of circumstance and allowed him to see two souls in need. In Mrs. Brittany, unusual warmth was the sweet essence of living; outside of her was the cold stench of minutes and hours he could not control. Deeper in Mrs. Brittany was the celebration of life and the emptiness of a thousand poems; outside of her was the scaly carcass of discarded facts, that perhaps he had, in fact, given up on his dreams, was a hopeless underachiever, that he no longer cared to be great, to be free to be the best artist in the world.

Mrs. Brittany was a New Orleans, a new world, he could enter; own, if only briefly, one who could give him back the dreams denied him by the incessant voodoo culminating at Jackson Square. In Mrs. Brittany was the moist deepness of a passion that left him lightheaded, bewildered, relieved and, yes, loved. And now everything and every moment outside of her was a dry love in blank verse.

The woman whose very essence gyrated beneath him was the voice of the canvas to a painter's brush, saying, "Let me bring out the best in you; please bring out the best in me!" She was the creator of pink and of roses and of song, the goddess of passion and of the tree of knowledge of good and evil. Her touch upon his lower back made him whole.

Almost as if she had found the cue card she had lost before, as she experienced his hot life in the flesh—and was reminded how all life flows—she whispered in his ear, "Let every heart that knoweth love say, '*Amen*' and '*Amen*.'"

And, on the third day, Mrs. Brittany once again appealed to her lover, who now looked at her through eyes of pity. For the first time, he broke down into tears.

"But you're not well," he repeated.

"Please, Trent. Don't pull this little boy act with me," she pleaded, her own eyes watery, swollen.

"I am not pulling a little-boy act! You tell me that you are dying of adeno—"

"Adenocarcinoma."

"I don't give a damn about pronouncing it!" he shouted. "You tell me you're dying of cancer of the pancreas, and I'm supposed to make love to you like nothing is new? I have a heart, you know."

"I know you do, sweetheart—"

"Why'd you do it? Tell me why you did it?" He tried to control his trembling voice, but could not.

"Why'd I do *what*?"

"You knew what the deal was ... and ... and you went on and let me fall in love with you. That was a cruel thing to do, Crystal. I'm not some little boy, and you know it. I'm a man who has a heart, who, who got caught with his guards down."

Wild birds echoed above the shack where, inside, the first man in the history of its existence cried. The radio and the static with which it transmitted jazz down from New Orleans had been silenced since she first decided to tell him of her plight. The room harbored a killer calmness that ripped from within until a deafening moan slashed the tranquility.

"God! Crystal? Are you all right?"

She wrapped her arms around her waist as if she was giving herself a hug.

"Baby, please tell me that you're all right!" Trent begged. She began to breathe in short pants. He noticed a tinge of yellowness in her eyes. Holding her out of love over lust, he finally realized that she had also lost a lot of weight.

"Trent?"

"Yes, sweetie."

"Please forgive me, sugar. I never wanted to take your humanity away. I didn't mean to make you feel like some animal being kept around for breeding. I just didn't want to be alone."

"I won't leave you."

"Hold me," she said, beginning to shake. "Oh, God. I hurt so badly. Please, just hold me. Hold me."

***

Trent started his Crystal Brittany collection a year following Mrs. Brittany's untimely death. It became his most successful body of work to date. His painting of a classy black woman horizontally suspended between the past and future sold for over one million dollars. It was a phenomenal work, even if he had slept with a prominent art dealer to promote it. Nonetheless, Mrs. Brittany had provided him with the finances and the wherewithal to succeed, so he decided to meet her halfway. Her lawyers also connected him with an ambitious agent, who helped create a network and market for his work that allowed him to move away from the big cities. He decided to return to the mocking African American motherland—Alabama.

He taught two art classes as an adjunct professor at Ebonia College to help out, but it definitely wasn't for the money. Being less than two hours from Atlanta allowed him to avoid that city's pathetic pretentiousness while also cementing his access to a world-class airport featuring flights to any destination in the world.

"You must really like the Whisky Sour concoction here," I said to Trent as we were preparing to leave. I closed my brown journal and tied up its two straps into a tight, almost non-existent bow. As I looked down at the book, I had to admit it to myself. I really loved my journal. It had all the intricacies of work from the 18th century, the fancy stitching, the slight but distinct bas relief-like floral prints throughout. Even the pages had the pseudo appearance of aged paper.

"Man, it's a mean Whisky Sour," Trent eventually responded. "I've got to hand it to him, even though he switches up the recipe on me sometimes. I especially like it when he adds a bit of maple syrup and uses the Crown Royal ... *balanced*, that's it."

He took a final sip. "You've sure been scratching in that damn pad a lot tonight, professor. What in hell are you working on?"

"A professor's work is never done," I said. "When I think about something I can do to help a student at the College, I have to write it down. I was also making a note of some of those eating places you visited back in New Orleans."

"I see," said Trent, perhaps one drink beyond caring. "Those students are lucky to have you."

Chapter 7 – Ruth's Tale

I was the only one at The Chinaberry Tree who knew what was going on between Ruth and her boss, a man she always called "The African." She even had cried on my shoulders a few times. We would talk for hours, I would offer logic, and she would accept it, but nothing ever changed. I knew she felt like trash, and I was afraid to tell her what I really thought: that she was a victim of her own greed and selfishness. Instead, I quietly listened to her scenarios with empathy, and a little longing. She never seemed to notice or care about my journal.

"Thou shalt have no other gods before me. Say it!"

"Please," pleaded a pleasant-looking, though slightly plump, Director of Marketing. "Can't we just do it normally?"

But The African would not hear of it. Educated, pompous, reverent and self-convinced that he was appealing, hung—and beyond denial, he slapped her buttocks and shouted at her to say the commandment as he thrust himself into her.

"Thou shalt have no other gods before me," she succumbed in almost a whisper. She clinched the sheets in her hands and, in a mighty, earth-shattering lunge forward, she fell upon her stomach, among what seemed to be a score of pink and lavender pillows. A small tear began to swell in her left eye as she thought of how far she had come to sink so low.

She was dying inside even as this live rage was pounding away inside of her like a crazed jackal. So many people, so many friends were so proud of her, she thought as she listened to The African make hissing sounds, his stomach now a turbulent river upon her lower back, as she heard the rodeo slaps to her buttocks harder and harder, and as he asked her again, "Who's God, good stuff?"

She tried to remain reticent, to bear the price for her successful climb like a woman. Another fierce, jolting slap made her whimper. "I said—Who's God?"

"You are," she answered.

This had become a common occurrence and what started out as a mere sexual agreement between two needing, aching adults had somehow grown one-sided, repugnant and demeaning. Word even had begun to traverse the small company in Saxonville that she was the President's ass. She also had begun to notice that some of her colleagues could no longer look her directly in the eyes.

Early in her bizarre relationship with The African, she had tried to convince herself that she was in love with him. When it became too incomprehensible that one could actually love so heartless a human creature, such Ivy League scum, she then tried to tell herself that she was in love with his power.

At first she had enjoyed the way she had managed to lure the thoughts of this pseudo-intellectual, phony neo-conservative away from his script at the meaningless meetings he periodically called for his staff. She then maneuvered her placement on ad hoc committees, took on leadership roles no one else wanted, and then somehow managed to get selected as the liaison between all groups and committees and The African.

The fact that he was married was only a minor technicality for Ruth Hightower. Smart, powerful, intelligent men of stature could not be held to the same mundane standards as their fellow men of plebeian balls. For too long she had comforted herself by the notion that at least she was screwing an Ivy League "somebody" and not some half-ass, country simpleton from Tuskegee or Morehouse. Still, she could not ignore the fact that she was indeed "getting screwed," nor that her friends who actually had married "nobodies" did not seem to have problems sleeping at night. Their men probably did not ask them, "Who's God?"

"Slide back," she heard The African command. She quietly obliged. Then he reached underneath her to rub her right breast. "Whose stuff is this?" he asked.

"Yours, big thang," she answered as they had rehearsed,

getting sicker on her stomach with each pulsation of their hatemaking.

"Yes!" he repeated rhythmically. "*Ooo*, you're good. Now, throw it back." Like a helpless love puppet, she continued to succumb to his demands and somehow managed the audacity to pretend that she was still in control of the situation.

In her quest for position, she knew she had sold out the absolute power of pure, unadulterated work ethic for a position for which she was not qualified and in which no support staffers would ever adequately assist her.

The African—it was no big secret—was an egotistical fool, a buffoon, a Napoleon III, and a charlatan who often held his black business hostage to assert his own selfish special interests. He ignored customer concerns, watched good staffers leave, and had nerve enough to publicly advertise that the company was "a quality firm" that people "should be honored to simply be associated with."

And now, here she was, spread-eagled and ogled, butt-naked in front of The African like a Thanksgiving turkey. What kept the tear from eventually falling was his "I'm never giving this pussy up." She knew that it would be over soon, at least this particular act of humiliation. He would soon push down hard on her lower back to balance himself as he heaved away from her. Then he would quickly shower, dress himself, light a cigarette and rest himself on the loveseat on the opposite side of the hotel room.

During other times, he seemed to get a sordid thrill from wiping his privates on her underwear, then eventually leaving the room to take a long shower, as though he were attempting to wash himself clean of the scene, the room, the utter funk of the situation—and her. When he would finally finish showering, he would promptly dress, primp and preen before the mirror.

Of late, she began to marvel at the pathetic sight. He's actually *proud* of that humongous forehead, that fat-assed nose and those thick, monster lips, she would think to herself, just as she looked across the bed and over to the vanity where the fourth lover in her life stood.

By contrast, she looked very much like she felt—like a receptacle for toxic waste. She quietly prayed for him to say something insensitive, anything, but to just leave to allow her time to recuperate from the massive hemorrhage of dignity.

Prior to his departure, he mumbled something about wanting a report on his desk by the following morning. She finally pulled herself up from the bed of shame, her buttocks sore and red from more than an hour of striking, her waist and lower back stinging from the scratches from The African's fingernails.

She fought her way into the shower, hoping to somehow rid herself of The African as she had countless times before. The water ran over her shoulders in steady blasts, and she closed her eyes, listened to the sound of the water hitting her yellow skin, the smell of the steam reincarnating fragrance and filth.

Ruth thought of her modest, almost sacrosanct upbringing and almost immediately began to cry. This time, like so many others before it, she felt sorry for herself, contemplated killing herself, killing someone.

She gained her composure, however, dried herself off, dressed comfortably and sat down on the bed to make a telephone call, likely to a man who knew how to treat women, one who was a devoted friend who could be counted on to quietly listen, to be trustworthy and understand.

Chapter 8 – Bo Willie's Tale

Bo Willie often talked to The Chinaberry Tree gang about the 'fucked up' childhood he had. He would never go into details. One night, I continued to sit at the long bar of his club as most of the patrons were beginning to leave. He usually refused to drink while he worked the bar, but tonight I noticed that he had downed a few shots of straight gin. When the last of the regulars had left the bar, he began to open up to me. This surprised me, mostly because I was never really sure what he thought of me.

This was the first of seven occasions that he descended into a lower room, taking me into the depths with him, whether I wanted to take the ride or not. On most occasions, the darkened spaces involved his time in Vietnam as a soldier of Charlie Company in 1968. We'd talk for what seemed like hours about how his part in the My Lai Massacre destroyed his remaining belief in God.

"I saw how evil moves on dat bloody road," Bo Willie said, shaking his head, holding back a tear. "Sometimes you see dat devil in yo' fellow soldiers, and sometimes you be fightin' to pull him out of yo'self. All dem innocent folks. Where was they god? Where was *ours*?"

Often, the intensity of our conversations caused my psyche to ache as though I had been kidnapped for days. He would take me into such cruel spaces, depleting my stores emotionally, mentally and spiritually. I could only assume that he definitely wanted me to feel every pain he had felt, to become snagged as he had in the jungles not too far from Saigon.

"'Nam was the answer to da black man's push for civil rights in 'merica, hopin' he and da redneck would find a way to an honorable death," Willie surmised.

Even stateside, Bo Willie remained a walking, talking time bomb at a minimum of three full-hour blocks, psychologically three whole days in a seven-day cycle. He could have made it back with his mind intact, he said, but having been burdened with the layer of black skin had made the return to humanity way too difficult. There were too many enemies to fight all at once. There were nights when he thought that even the moon was mocking him.

Before Vietnam, Bo Willie had simply been a black man in America, tasked with proving his humanity to a white man who proved anything but human. His fragile mental state was a dingy glass house scratched up by the hypocrisy of his momma's religion, the ambitions of scores of neighborhoods redlined into tight blocks, a horrendous but necessary history, and the shoddily concocted notion of decency at all costs.

Yes. Stateside, he had been forced to convince himself that, even if the white man often didn't act so, he was still a human being. But in the throes of war, Bo Willie soon realized that the inhuman human was utterly other-worldly. There was no line between man and animal except the thread called survival.

Some of my visits alone with Bo Willie delved into his numerous psychological scars, formed from having survived when others he felt more deserving of life had died like swollen dogs in a strange land. There were times at The Chinaberry Tree when I dared not pull out my journal for fear he'd mistake any move for the Viet Cong.

We constantly stumbled in and out of his PTSD episodes, his survivor's guilt, and his incessant desire to recapture the human spirit, especially when war had meant acknowledging that nothing separated man from beast. Bo Willie said that in Vietnam he saw, with lightening speed, all that America had done to black people over the course of hundreds of years. Bullied relocations and wholesale destruction of communities, mutilation, group and individual torture and abuse, indiscriminate murder amid a state that mocked the mere notion of justice, massacres at will, and countless rapes that produced thousands of yellow half-satans that the black community was obliged to raise within the confines of its walls.

"We was too stupid to even think dat we all—black, white and other—had been thrown ina pit of genocide. It was da same pit us called hell back in da States," Bo Willie said. "I betcha a quarta of da 'merican soldiers was fucked up from mainlinin' heroin."

This visit, however, was a little different. It took a strange turn. On this particular day, he told me the story of a little Bo Willie who was trembling and holding on to the leg of a mid-century modern, stick-leg kitchen table. He talked about how that child had cried as his uncle beat him mercilessly with a thick, leather belt, a before-the-country-lost-its-meaning-of-what-was-genuine-and-real belt, and the kind of belt that could pull a tractor-trailer: a 1958 belt of unspoiled cowhide.

"Stop that damn crying," said a gross caricature of a man named Jeremiah, who drew back deep into the never-never land to which his mind sometimes traveled and pulled forth his arm into the present against the fragile realities of a five-year-old's legs, back and head. Little Bo Willie, it seemed, had committed the most hideous of crimes.

"Why can't you eat it?" the uncle asked for the seventh time, referring to the deep dark brown chocolate icing he himself had etched away from the white cake with his teeth, leaving it in a jagged line on a plate for his uppity nephew to eat. Watching on was the uncle's daughter, a senseless doo-wop type, who either loved her father in spite of his trips into insanity or because of the generosity of his returns.

When Bo Willie declined to eat the chocolate icing, the walls came tumbling down. The boy immediately realized that his uncle perceived his refusal as an indication that the child had the audacity to presume that Uncle J was an inferior being, a nobody.

Throughout the early 1960s everyone still knew that feelings of inferiority were only natural when dealing with a white society to whom one merely paid rent. It also was a time when it was much easier to be fully insane and "away" than sane and thought a fool by people who controlled both your world and theirs.

Uncle J, as Bo Willie sometimes hesitantly called him, had been in and out of overcrowded and dilapidated state mental institutions designed for blacks. The facilities were an indirect correlation to what those in control thought about the needs of black people for centuries. Shoddy infrastructure, inadequate heat during the winters, rows of institutional iron-frame beds in rows throughout a large room, and modest attempts at sanitation, with always a whiff of piss.

His sister, Bo Willie's mother, had somehow convinced his father to allow Uncle J to live with them in Alabama. But Bo Willie's father and Uncle J never got along. Perhaps it was because of understandable personality conflicts, or perhaps it was because Uncle J reminded his father too much of Bo Willie's mama: the wide, flaring nostrils; the terse, smart-ass responses to mundane questions; and their constant taking up for one another. Maybe these factors help explain why the kid's father hated Jeremiah in spite of the fact that Uncle J was his wife's favorite brother.

But hating Uncle J was an easy—even natural—job at that point in time among a set of men in their humble abode. His bold mid-African features would not yield to any form of European assimilation and his unyielding hair was an embarrassment to those respectable Negro men who had somehow and for some reason redirected their lives toward proving to whites—who still despised them nonetheless—that they were, in fact, okay. It was a helluva mission, one that often required purging any number of traitors to the cause.

Bo Willie's father also would have been justified in hating Uncle J for a much more logical reason: the man was crazy. And, of all the things an uneducated Negro man had to contend with in the late 1950s and early 1960s, a freeloading, crazy bastard who always sided with your frigid bitch of a wife did not make the list.

Uncle J's predicament was no less difficult. He was a man on an expensive, extended voyage, who had to return too frequently to pay the price for lesser trips—wife, children, home—about which he could conjure little recollection of taking. He was a man who was always marching along walls he had constructed. Whether he was on the inside or outside of those walls was purely a matter of perspective.

Far too often Uncle J went on yet another excursion, somewhere deep in the woodlands of western Mississippi of 1925, where the nights opened wide and wanton to the penetration of fireflies and half-naked black bucks running across an expanse of cotton fields of a late and chilly October night. Among the thicket, a sharecropping redneck named Hopewell pushed a little Negro boy's head down to his groin. His friend Hamilton had escaped.

"Put it back in yo' mouth!" the redneck repeated, bringing a fist down on the boy's naked back. "You betta not say a damn thing 'bout this boy, y' hear?" Not wanting his mother or his sister to die and physically out-mastered, the twelve-year-old succumbed, hoping to soon be about his father's business.

"Put it back in your mouth!" Uncle J shouted at Bo Willie, punching him in the back of his head with his fist. He continued beating Bo Willie like a madman, his damaged brain short-circuiting between past and present. His daughter, frightened, yielded to nervous titters of laughter. He picked the boy up by one arm, high into the air and lashed him several times with the thick belt, using all of his might. The dingy, yellow kitchen began to swerve as the crazed man continued to beat Bo Willie for 'acting uppity.'

Little Bo Willie thought Uncle J was about to throw him through the kitchen window. He held the boy by his small arm, suspending him in midair over the kitchen table, walloping him senselessly. Between the blows, the swinging, the rain from his eyes, the laughter of a helpless witness, Bo Willie, still swinging, looked over the stove, through the flimsy curtains and out the window. Beyond it, for a split second, he thought he saw a large moon with a smirk on its face.

"When I say eat something," screamed Uncle J, "I mean for you to eat it, little nigga!" With a last burst of strength, Uncle J hurled Bo Willie under the kitchen table like a fallen angel. Landing by a table leg, Bo Willie begged the man to leave him alone, and he agreed to eat as he was told. Trembling, as much from fear as from a failure to garner the *why* of the situation, Bo Willie began to eat the chocolate icing that Uncle J had only moments earlier spit out to avoid having trouble with his "sugar."

As the whimpering boy slowly ate, coming to terms between sobs with the notion that he would have to face the troubles of the world on his own, Uncle J came behind him, with a breath bathed in snuff and buttermilk, and placed his right hand on Bo Willie's small, shaking left shoulder. He lowered his head down by the boy's and closed his eyes.

"That's it, little nigga," he cooed. "You like that, don't you?" When the boy finished eating most of the icing, reclaiming the lost melanin that had led to the necessity of this lesson, Uncle J raised himself from his semi-crotched position, walked through the kitchen's off-white screened door, onto the small back porch of the little brown house and paused at the steps. The last of the green grass was still hanging around in the backyard.

His sister's house was on an alley, or half-street. It also was expertly situated in and ever-destined for the colored subdivision of a colored section within a white town in a proud white state in a white country leasing space within a colored world. Uncle J hesitated a bit as he walked down the cement steps and turned right, stumbling all the way to the incredibly large fig tree. Just above his head, he placed his left hand on the high limb that towered over the chain link fence. He placed his right hand on another large limb that brushed against the window of the house's only bathroom. He looked out toward a wooded area, from which traveled the sounds of distant peacocks. He then hung his head, low and reverent, like a blue-eyed Jesus in the Kress store picture, and cried.

When Bo Willie's parents finally arrived home, a little late from work, Uncle J and his simple daughter greeted them but left quickly. Before getting himself settled to assist with dinner, Bo Willie's father noticed that his son did not seem his usual, happy self.

"What's the matter, li'l man?" he asked.

"Nothing," replied the boy.

"Come here. What's the matter?" asked the father again. "You know you can tell me," he added, sensing something, wanting to believe something was awry with that "other Negro" who lived in his house.

"Uncle J beat me," Bo Willie finally confessed.

"What were *you* doing?" interrupted his mother, poised for a reason to commence a beating all her own.

"What he doin' beatin' on you?" asked his father. The kitchen was still with anticipation. For his father, who seldom won an argument at home, even when he was right, this situation might prove to be the straw that would land J's ass back in a mental institution. For his mother, the same situation might be the very act proving her brother's sense of responsibility, packaged in the disciplining of a child who sorely needed it.

"I wouldn't eat icin' he bit off of," said Bo Willie.

"What the fuck he doin' beatin' on Bo Willie?" shouted Willie Sr. "Hell, he don't do nothin' to hiz own crazy-ass kids. Who in the fuck wants to eat offa somethin' he has had in his damn, stank-ass mouth?"

"Aw, shit, man," screamed Bo Willie's mother. "That boy done done somethin' he didn't have no business, and J oughta whip him."

"When that son of a bitch bring hiz ass back here, we'll see who oughta be doin' some whippin'," promised Willie Sr. He motioned for Bo Willie to come toward him.

"Come here, li'l man. Raise up your shirt."

Bo Willie stood up from the kitchen table and slowly did as his father told him. He could feel his father's rage before he had said a word.

The boy's back was overlaid with imprints of a series of crosses, from the bottom of his neck and extending down to his buttocks. Three Greek crosses were strewn over his shoulder blades, Latin crosses were etched out his mid-back and there were Scandinavian crosses and Lithuanian crosses mixed throughout.

"Look at this! Look at all these damn strap marks! I wanna see that motherfucker!" Bo Willie's mama ignored his father's stares and protests and proceeded to change her clothes to begin dinner, although Willie Sr. was the real cook of the family. Willie Sr. made her find and bring the Jergens lotion.

About an hour later, Uncle J returned alone and was immediately approached by Bo Willie's father in the kitchen. As argument quickly ensued, Willie Sr. sent the boy to another part of the four-room house. But when the three voices began to escalate, Bo Willie ran to the entrance of the kitchen and saw the three-sided pyramid. His mother was armed with a black cast iron skillet and was indicating her readiness to launch a homerun with his father's head. Uncle J, for his part, was holding up his fists as if preparing for self-defense.

"Motherfucker, don't you be beatin' on dat boy!" shouted Willie Sr., who formed the base of the triangle.

"You kiss my ass!" answered Uncle J, positioned at the top right.

Willie Sr. rushed for the double-blade ax he kept on top of the white wood kitchen cupboard on the wall parallel to the refrigerator, but Uncle J grabbed the ax with his left hand on the wood handle near the blade and the other hand just slightly above Willie Sr.'s right hand on the lower handle. The two men tussled, and the fragile wood floor beneath them struggled to hold up their weight, which was the humane thing to do. The feet of the humans, however, pounded the floor mercilessly like incoherent African drums echoing in the deep chambers of a slave ship. The men knocked the kitchen table into the loins of his mother, pinning her "crazy, hoodoo ass", as the father had shouted, into the corner formed by the sink and back window, weakening the screened door. Uncle J managed to break the upper end of the ax away from Willie Sr.'s grip, still a little slippery from the lotion, and brought the ax down on the right corner of Willie Sr.'s head.

Bo Willie wailed and nearly fainted when he saw a spurt of dark red blood trickle down his father's head. Fortunately, it was hardly more than a flesh wound, but Willie Sr., after staggering back a few paces, quickly ceased the physical confrontation, collected himself and, like a man who had just found Jesus, walked erectly to the telephone and called the police.

When the black policemen assigned to Negro matters arrived, Willie Sr. was there to meet them and promptly told them that his brother-in-law had beat his son unnecessarily and—when he, as befitting a concerned father, had approached the abuser about it, his brother-in-law had—in a fit of crazed rage—struck him in the head with an ax in an attempt to murder him.

The policemen came and then asked to see the ax. Fresh bloodstains. Willie Sr. then went on to explain how Uncle J had been in and out of state mental institutions and told them that the man was indeed "crazy." Meanwhile, Bo Willie's mother disputed the claims against her brother. Within minutes, Willie Sr., Bo Willie and his upset mama—who kept murmuring that Uncle J "should have killed him"—all watched Uncle J as he was carried off peacefully in the backseat of the police car.

"Don't worry, J," said the mother and wife. "I'll get you out."

But Uncle J was never seen again, at least, not by Bo Willie nor Willie Sr., and that was all that really mattered. It was like that for black men: whether you stayed or went away, it really didn't matter, since prayers always canceled each other out.

After the incident, Bo Willie's father seemed to age as if someone had cast an evil spell on him. Perhaps this was a proper tribute to questionable liquor purchased from the homes of too many church-going bootleggers. Perhaps it could have been due in part to decades of unfiltered cigarettes. But more likely his cancerous grays were caused by the demonstrated betrayals and constant frustrations from a wife who never really learned how to love, not even by this, her third marriage.

Illiterate, the father had mastered the art of writing his name to cash his payroll checks and could follow a map to any location in the continental U. S. Willie Sr. was a man who wanted only simple pleasures, was basically a kind man who, perhaps, drank too much, but who also talked with reason and cunning despite any given condition of his liver.

Bo Willie could not understand why his mother never seemed to love his father. But, because he loved her, he always tried. He reasoned that it had something to do with what the bootlegging Miz Lou would moan when his father would be the lone customer at her house. Usually after he had downed his second drink of straight gin, Willie Sr. would tell his son to go into the living room to watch the big screen, black and white TV, while he went upstairs to talk about "church business" with Miz Lou.

Sometimes he'd watch a western or some goody-goody show like "Tammy" or "Dobie." But in the distance he would hear the sound of an old spring mattress, like the way it sounded when he and his cousin Mane jumped up and down on their grandmother's bed in the country.

"You love my stuff, don't ya?" he would hear Miz Lou ask his father from the upper room in the neighborhood known as The Bottom. His father's reply was mostly indistinguishable, although sometimes he could hear his father tell her to "remember Bo Willie."

Upon leaving, Bo Willie once asked his father why church business had to be so noisy.

"Prayer is like that," his father replied.

Willie Sr. lived a life in mockery of the church. Born, too, in Mississippi, he always told stories about his childhood days, times when pale, white ghosts would chase colored children through the cornfields. He also talked about a "mean-assed" stepfather who would dig up his stepchildren's buried dimes and spend them on whiskey. He viewed churchgoers as empty fakes who would be pure demons if they didn't have to go back to church constantly for refills.

Bo Willie's mother, on the other hand, was a staunch Christian woman of the worst, self-righteous, stubborn kind. To punish her husband for any of his countless atrocities, she would withhold sex and invite her friends over to talk about what it was like to have a bastard for a husband. To show that he really did not give a damn, he would take a nap in the tiny living room at the front of the small house, but not before unzipping his pants and pulling his penis out to swing freely as he snored. If his mother had failed but once to halt her gossiping wenches before their departure via the living room, it could have been either the shock or thrill of their insignificant lives.

This humiliated the hell out her, for although she wanted very much not to respond to this indecency, she had to concede that what he had was hers even if she decided not to use it. She also hated that she could never quite seem to use his penis to control him as she had, for the lion's share, in her first two marriages. Despite her incessant efforts to manage him, he remained outside of her clutches. But during those rare moments when she was in his, he didn't let her forget who was in control. He left her lightheaded and fighting her desires for more.

These and countless other escapades of intense love and sizzling hatred had plagued Bo Willie throughout his entire life. They literally deprived him of a childhood and, coupled with the insanity of Vietnam, forever impaired his claim to his rightful piece of humanity.

Chapter 9
Reverend Wright's Tale

"Memo from the Director's Office," proclaimed a young braided, paper-thin volunteer as she placed the photocopied announcement on top of Buddy's "in" tray. She looks anemic, Buddy thought, and he watched her walk down the narrow hallway leading from his office to the cage of Abraham Tinker, the director of the Senior Center. He picked up the memorandum and began to read:

The Office of the Director is pleased to announce the appointment of Ms. Sarah Oldham to the important position of Special Assistant to the Director for Community Relations and Special Events.

In this capacity, Ms. Oldham will advise the Director on pertinent issues and concerns pertaining to the Center and its role in the community, as well as assist and represent the Office of the Director in the planning and coordination of various events. These will include, but not be limited to, the Easter and Summerfest, Thanksgiving and Christmas festivities.

Please join me in congratulating Ms. Oldham on her new duties in the Office of the Director.

"Time for fertilizer already?" Buddy commented to himself, returning the letter to the "in" tray. As he walked over to the adjoining office to prepare himself a cup of coffee, he heard his phone ring.

"Hello."

"Buddy?"

"Yeah."

"Reverend Wright," said the tenor voice. Reverend Wright was his best friend, but he always, out of habit, identified himself. "Did you read that bull they were passing out?"

"I did," answered Buddy. "I think Sarah is making a mistake by associating with Abraham like that. "Can't tell her shit, though. She's another one of those fiercely independent sistahs who're determined to get theirs, no matter what. Ain't no limit to the crap she'll put up with just to fool herself into thinking she's arrived."

"You know, I've wondered if I'd do what she's doing if the tables were turned," commented Reverend Wright, a jackleg preacher whose day job found him as The Senior

Center's spiritual advisor. He was basically a good guy, although he deluded himself into thinking he could perform dual roles as both shepherd of the flock and wayward lamb. Away from the pulpit, his wanton familiarity with the weaker sex was second only to any leading gynecologist. He prided himself on knowing where to touch a woman "to make her climb the walls."

Those women who "did not see him like that" were only too happy to climb the walls within a moist, hot church on those humid, down Deep South Sunday mornings, when souls were left out in the open and emotional wounds were allowed to come to a head. Somewhere, right in the middle of the sheaths separating the stoic realities of a broken Promised Land and the drunken passion of better days ahead, Reverend Wright entered the Amen sisters in a way they could never, would never, reveal. He sensually massaged their troubled spots, thoroughly washed away their dreads, neatly closed all of the doors behind him, and quietly left them to drain. As far as he and Sarah were concerned, it was difficult to tell who hated and loved the opposite sex more.

"Do what she's doing?" queried Buddy. "You mean sleeping around to get ahead?"

"Yeah, you know," Reverend Wright fiddled at his desk with a chain of paperclips. "Suppose some nice looking—or homely looking, for that matter—woman was my supervisor and it became absolutely clear that I could get ahead by going to bed with her. I've asked myself if I'd do it."

"Well, how did your *self* respond?" asked Buddy, now forced to consider the scenario himself.

"I'd have boss lady's kneecaps boxing her ears," retorted Reverend Wright. After a brief silence, the two burst into a fit of laughter as the image overwhelmed them.

"And you're supposed to be a reverend?" Buddy asked in jest. "Man, does the Baptist ordaining committee need a refresher course!"

"What? Did I say something wrong?" teased Reverend Wright, lighting himself a cigarette and opening a window to his small office. "I'm a man first, no? What about you? What would you do?"

"I don't know," Buddy replied. "I would seriously think about it. But, you know me; I'd rather have my freedom. I just couldn't have some woman snapping her fingers and telling me what to do."

"You're looking at it all wrong," explained the often-wrong Reverend Wright. "If you work it in the right way, you'd get all she has and not have to do anything for her. In fact, it would be no big deal to find her looking for you with a flashlight at noon on the interstate."

"Where do you come up with this shit?"

Reverend Wright regarded Buddy as a true friend, one he could confide in about his weaknesses without fear of being judged. With Buddy he could relax, just as he had on countless evenings with the wives of other men. And while he knew Buddy undoubtedly thought he should curb his appetite for the illicit somewhat, Reverend Wright found in Buddy a shoulder upon which to rest his mind from the lengthy stints of deceit.

But Reverend Wright still found deceit a very bitter word to swallow. He preferred to think of his seminal depths as an interchange of needs. Women, he honestly believed, were knowingly open for lies, preferred lies as well as pretending there should be more to a relationship than wet sheets. He viewed them as the enemy he confronted each day and night on a battlefield, an awesome foe whose skills mirrored his own, whose cunning was just as crafty, and whose insidious lust was just as impermeable.

"But seriously," continued Reverend Wright, changing his tone, "I think airhead Sarah is getting in over her head." He turned around in his stool so that he could look out of his third floor window to see the TeenPower Center across town. It was the only such center located on a black college campus.

"She actually thinks she has become a part of Abraham's circle," said Buddy. "But, Sarah—as I see it—will never be more than his piece of ass."

"And what an ass!" added Reverend Wright. "If she'd just let me draw from that well one time, I know I'd 'come whole.'"

"Watch it, Reverend. What you'd 'come is unemployed," replied Buddy, stealing a look down the hallway. "You know damn well Abraham would debone your ass if he even thought you were messing with his stuff."

"He's too old to catch me. Anyway, since tithes have been falling off, some, and since the good Reverend needs his day job, they both can consider her booty safe for now," laughed the man of the cloth. "I gotta go. I have revival tonight."

Chapter 10 – David's Tale

All educated white folks seemed to have a great appreciation for Negro spirituals, David once surmised as the white and blue-haired choral director led the mostly Caucasian chorus in a repeat of Tillman Lawson's "In the Plains with God." As one of only about ten blacks in the massive group, David always wondered just which large white church or organization the high school group would be visiting next. Integration, it appeared, then, always meant going to them.

Having been born with a veil and cloak with the weight of old folks' unrealized hopes and dreams, David's shoulders seemed to droop from pressure. Yet, the elders mistook his plainness and humility as the divine façade of a warrior angel who would someday send white folks a-running.

No matter how frustrated he grew at having to find his way at night through strange white neighborhoods or at mustering small talk following performances, he managed to completely lose himself—despite the Southern twang of his peers—and among voices singing "Sho Nuf Good News." Because his own view of what it meant to be black was only limited to how it made him feel when he was occasionally called "nigger," he could not understand—it was impossible to comprehend—the necessity of spiritual escapism.

As long as he had to deal with the weighted reality of being a black boy in such a mediocre Southern town, he could never know the alternative challenges of simply growing to be a Christian or an American.

Through Lawson, though, were the intoxicating wings with which to fly away to another place, another country, mind soaring high—just above His head—with a tolerated African co-existence. But how could he lose himself, totally, among a field of blue eyes and striped rugby shirts? Would they understand if he sang a bit too loudly or with too much fervor? Would the French baritone left of him, the Irish kid in front of him or the Jewish kid to the far right of him understand the price of this black boy's ticket, paid by the millions of bodies thrown atop the Atlantic? Or, would his white peers only smell the subtle but revealing poignancy of a different Royal Crown in his kinky hair? Would they be reminded of and offended by the cologne he had purchased for two bucks from the Diamond on 15th and 29th? What did they really think of him, expect of him? Was he simply being tolerated as a silently acknowledged source of historical anguish? And, with so many blue eyes feeling such unease, brought on by his sheer presence, how could his brown eyes envision the world encapsulated in the singing of his own song?

But a flurry of other concerns, too, prevented David from losing himself while riding on the chariot that black fairy godfather Lawson had provided for him. It was impossible to believe in himself because there was no concept of self. Because there was no concept of self, there was no place inside of him for aspiration. Thus, his was a dangerously futile existence—one hopelessly tagged to gaining open acceptance from those who would unequivocally despise him.

Then, one day it happened. The really dark old folks call it "The Spirit." Perhaps he saw himself as the talisman his grandfather saw in him. Nonetheless, how innocuous elderly black people see it and how the cosmos portrays it are essentially the same. For both worlds, a blinding display of colors simultaneously radiated from and were funneled back to his third eye, the pineal gland, forcing a massive white beam and pathway for solo flight.

Whatever manner by which it revealed itself to other dimensions, it definitely hit David like an archaic slingshot whose only purpose was to down a boastful Philistine. He was singing, on the back row, with Pennon Burkhalter next to him on the right and with Newt Stein on the left. The choir was singing Lawson's "I'm Going Home to Live with God." It was a song about gaining refuge from suffering, about being 'done' with the world's problems. It was a song, at once, too laden with prerequisites in the curriculum of life for any lone black high school senior. But he felt The Spirit.

No mo' weepin' and a'wailin' ... No mo' weepin' and a'wailin' ... No mo' weepin' and a'wailin' ... I've gone to live wid God!

The experience had become so insanely intense that the words were meshing with the room's acoustics like softened sweet peas bursting on the tongue. Little old white ladies politely smiled as the sound of the chorus caressed them like a Yerby novel. David slowly, uncontrollably, began to lift his arms as if he were suspended from a cross, or walking between heavenly bodies on a beam of light. He started to mimic a celestial bird in flight. His voice began to soar above the stratosphere.

I want to meet my father
I want to meet my father
I want to meet my father
I've gone to live with God.

The choir director took notice and was shocked at first, for David had always been the quiet, unassuming student. She did not know what to make of him. Then a broad smile flashed on her face, and she began to direct as she never had before. The boy had become proof that they had soul! It was as if, through her constant fascination with the Negro folk melody, she had somehow recaptured The Spirit. It was in David! While they did not fully capture the richness of the dialect, the choir performed admirably and even received a standing ovation.

People came up to talk to him following the performance. Suddenly, they wanted to get to know him better, to know who his folks were.

What could he tell them, really? That his father was ranting to anyone in the neighborhood who would listen that his wife was using voodoo on him? That at one time his father had bought an old school bus, had installed a stove and bed in it, had parked it right in front of the damned house, and had moved in it? Could he tell them that his mother worked as a maid, probably for one of them?

Whatever spirit he had had promptly left him, although he would later become addicted to it, find himself longing for refills and ever destined to horrible, crashing bouts of depression. His impression of Lawson, though, held constant, like Job. He wanted to know everything about him. He wanted to share those things that had gone into the making of a man who could compose such powerful joy and pain, capture the flesh-shearing pull between a world of seemingly innocuous pseudo-rationality and the mundane gamble of redemption.

When he learned that Lawson had attended a small university in the bowels of Alabama, he was determined to go there. He found the school to be everything he had longed to see in a school: hope, a deep-rooted sense of history, and the spirit of Africans who had flown before.

It was not long before he was able to see that his choral idol was more respected in the world than he was at the institution and in the community that had built itself around it. Upperclassmen referred to the small university as "The Museum" and spoke of the relics that it conveniently dusted off and pulled out for display—their predestined lives among them.

Indeed Lawson, the great Lawson, appeared as a treasured collectible that had been forgotten to be dusted and polished. In such a state he seemed politely unwelcome. Aging is the loin fruit of all that's vintage. But genius void of dignity and protection is an imposter to civility. Well into his nineties, Lawson appeared locked in a struggle to hold onto his dignity, alone. Most people David would come to know at The Museum would appear to be waging the same war.

Up until the time Lawson died, David unknowingly conducted an incessant love affair with The Museum, began dangerously clinging to its bosom in the late hours and yearning for more in the early mornings. Like an insect on a Venus flytrap, he had wandered a bit too close to The Museum, had allowed it to consume him and to drain him of his lifeblood. In the name of an unattainable and vague cause, he had unwittingly sold his soul. And now he, his friend Beth and everyone else with the misfortune of serving The Museum were no better off than common, ordinary street whores. He had lost his veil, his calling.

It is possible, it would seem, to be a whore for even an ostensibly noble cause, a harlot for the sake of the seductive safety of routine, or a mad mistress laboring largely with a life that is not a life.

The Museum, David's alma mater and Ebonia's largest employer, had become lifeless, colorless, thoughtless. People he once looked up to for their strength and courage were either fast retiring or closet basket cases. He hoped a new president's commitment to excellence and new blood would revitalize Ebonia's educational legacy of lifting the veil.

Chapter 11 – Crazy Hezekiah's Tale

The first set of blue eyes in a place have the added charge of proving there's a soul behind them. I guess that was part of my mission while in Ebonia. In addition to the usual philosophers and clowns at The Chinaberry Tree, however, there were a few people who were justifiably crazy. In other words, they had their papers. One such person was Crazy Hezekiah. He walked along the streets of Ebonia talking to himself, saying, "Poor me!" and answering his own questions. His matted hair had a personality all its own, and the funk that accompanied him sometimes joined in on his conversations.

The chronicles containing the exact story on Crazy Hezekiah were believed to be lost, perhaps with the burial of

Papa Schaumburg, the self-appointed Ebonia historian whose treasure of knowledge was never fully captured prior to his death seven years ago, when his stately home burned to the ground. He knew the ins and outs of every square inch of Ebonia. The true story, though, was still around, only trapped in bits and pieces in the collective memories of select Ebonians. Those precious fragments surfaced so randomly that they could rarely form a coherent story of a man whose first name was hopelessly tied to an adjective.

Somewhere back in time, before he had gone off the deep end, an 18-year-old Hezekiah of athletic build would help Papa Schaumburg with his records. He would sit on the porch of the Victorian-style home for hours during the day, reading over Papa Schaumburg's historical work. He'd also assist him in a basement that Schaumburg had made using the ample height underneath the home. There, Papa Schaumburg had collected what seemed like thousands of newspapers, old magazine articles and clippings sent to him from friends all over the world. Hezekiah's only complaint was that there was only dim light and an old oil lamp to read by. The college paid Schaumburg such a measly salary that he never entertained the notion of installing lights. Besides, he was doing the school a favor.

The perceived lack of a past, as it were, further condemned Crazy Hezekiah. Few knew that he remembered photographically almost all he had ever read in Schaumburg's basement. Instead, people jumped and became immediately uneasy whenever he approached them. In fact, he was the only other man in town who could silence Bo

Willie. Yet, owing to his "crazy" badge, he was accorded kid gloves around the village. When their money 'was kinda funny,' the two town whores gave him sex at a discount. But the badge also kept Crazy Hezekiah from being human. And, because he was not really human, no one ever really listened to what he had to say. No one tried to connect the dots to his many ramblings. Moreover, he was what older black folks used to call "tongued-tied." When he spoke, it sometimes seemed that his tongue was stuck to the bottom of his mouth. This and his odd demeanor made them discount his soliloquies as the babble of a lunatic.

Late one Friday evening, Crazy Hezekiah flung open the door of The Chinaberry Tree, causing the little bell above it to nearly fly off its hinges. "Poor me!"

"Evening," muttered Mr. Butler, impervious. Mr. Porter cleared his throat, a clear warning to his patrons that an alien had entered the premises. Of all the times Crazy Hezekiah could have brought his funky ass in for a damn drink, Mr. Butler and Mr. Porter both preferred that he show up on late, late Saturday evenings. Crazy Hezekiah *always* seemed to forget their gentlemen's agreement! A later entrance would have allowed them an opportunity to sterilize, pull out the cheap glasses and to pre-fumigate and post-fumigate the place.

Trent, David and a few other stragglers, who had all downed their drinks but were simply hanging on for the conversation, began to slowly bid their farewells, one by one.

"Look at the time," said Ruth Hightower, just stepping down from the bar after a Long Island Iced Tea. "I need to get on out of here." She paid Mr. Butler, tried to inconspicuously hold her nose to block the smell of the new client as she waited for her change to leave a tip, and then quickly went on her way, leaving her jacket with the small notepad and miniature tape recorder in its pockets. Ruth had resorted to jotting down more of her notes because of problems she was currently having cutting off the little device.

When Crazy Hezekiah was finally served, he almost was the last client in the bar. Mr. Porter had already closed the blinds and locked the doors. That was the signal that no other throats would be greased that evening.

"Okay," began Mr. Porter, throwing a napkin before Hezekiah that was stopped by a short, thick plastic glass. "What's it gonna be this time?"

"Gin," answered Crazy Hezekiah. "Poor me." As Mr. Porter hummed a tune, Crazy Hezekiah, almost on cue, began his silly soliloquy, the one everyone heard yet did not hear. His words were dismissed, along with his filth.

As the only white guy in the place on many occasions, I had developed a propensity for hearing while pretending not to be listening. On one such evening, I followed Crazy Hezekiah to a corner of the bar, where he seemed content to simply look out the window, just gazing off into the distance, his vision resting on a not-so-distant, transparent plane. Sometimes, his words were pure nonsense, but, to me, there was a fragment of a possibility that his nonsense was intentional, coded. On a rare situation or two, even I would be hard pressed to argue against anyone compelled to take him away in an off-white asylum straitjacket. On other equally rare occasions, though, I would mentally cut his canvas prison and allow him to breathe and sigh as I listened to his rantings.

One day, a day I'll never forget, I sat at a table behind Crazy Hezekiah on a gloomy day on March 3 around 7 p.m. For some reason, none of the regulars had wandered in. I took out my journal. Hezekiah was steadily drinking his botanical gin. He was talking as if someone or something else was at the table with him. He would pause, almost as though he was waiting on this other being to respond to him. It was so damn weird, and the shit went on for at least twenty to thirty minutes. There was no black dialect, and, except for tuning me out, along with everything else in the bar, Hezekiah seemed perfectly lucid. For the time, he was like some intergalactic attorney pleading for the continuance of mankind.

"I know you have been here for thousands of years," Crazy Hezekiah said to The Unknown, "but it is still too early to reveal your presence in the way you want to do it. You don't seem to get it. Why can't you get it? You are so advanced, on a totally different frequency. Yet, there is nothing I can even say to explain how far ahead you are." There was a pause. Crazy Hezekiah sipped his gin. The funk mirrored him. He then tilted his head upward in the manner religious people do when they are looking heavenward while extending their hands for grace and manna. But, given the conversation, Crazy Hezekiah's head gesture could have been likened to a wayward hologram attaching a hose to his frontal lobe, sending seductive light waves all the way back to the central sulcus.

"The collective psyche of earth would be short-circuited if you show up here now," the gin man pleaded. "We simply are not ready. Our entire way of life depends on us believing that we are the only ones in the universe. If you show up here now, people who think they own the world would be powerless. They only have enough weapons to destroy earth. How could they possibly understand your potential to eliminate entire galaxies?"

For the next seventy minutes, I heard Crazy Hezekiah respond, point by point, to The Unknown, who must have suggested that the world could benefit greatly from challenges to its religions and philosophies, the knocking over of its idolatrous monuments to fleeting not-so-ancient victories. Every triumph in human intellectual discourse and discovery—since the beginning of earth time—could be placed on The Unknown's memory stick, with room to spare for at least 337 other worlds in galaxies this earth will never, *ever* discover.

Crazy Hezekiah continued with his 'Why Earth?' stance. "Then start with the other 337," he said. They had. Then Crazy Hezekiah explained the level of cognitive dissonance, fear and existential anxiety, as well as the disrupting paradigm shift in human knowledge and politics.

The Unknown likely responded that politics wouldn't be anything to worry about, since the being Earth refers to as 'the white man' wouldn't be running shit.

"Help my human mind understand why you are doing this," Hezekiah asked. Then, The Unknown's answer could only be pieced together by way of Crazy Hezekiah's erratic responses.

"No," answered Crazy Hezekiah, his voice dropping in volume and with melancholy. "I *don't* understand the white man."

I heard him as he began to sob.

"You okay over there, son?" asked Mr. Porter.

Before making my way to the door, I spoke and gave a high five to Bo Willie, Trent, Brad and Isaac. I was scheduled to have dinner at Ethel's, and it was already 7:33 p.m. I didn't know what to expect from the elderly community leader, but she did not disappoint me.

Ethel's meal featured tantalizing cheddar-laden cauliflower soup with parsley, succulent lamb chops and a juicy slither of salmon, basmati rice, and buttery creamed spinach and sourdough bread with a French truffle butter. Afterward, we talked for hours about her childhood, her work with youth centers and even early Ebonia.

Following a fascinating visit, I ended the evening totally beat. I checked my fridge and decided to quench my thirst with a glass of apple juice before bed. As I stared at the popcorn ceiling, I began to recount the events of the day. The day's activities scrolled by, but my earlier time at The Chinaberry Tree stuck in my mind. Was Crazy Hezekiah actually speaking with someone? Why had he cried like a child?

I recall seeing a hologram of a man who easily could have passed for a 15th-century Moor, but in a futuristic sense. From head to toe, from his skin to his medieval-like garb to his flat shoes, the Moor became a levitating entity made up of a collage of symbolism. On his left wrist were miniscule flags of England and Morocco. The right wrist donned similarly sized flags of Guatemala and Canada. In the area of the right knee was an almost translucent flag of France, and on the left knee was one of Brazil. His left and right breasts flickered like a human billboard with the emblems of the United States to the Moor's right chest plate and Italy to his left, very close to his heart. But most disturbing was the most prominent national banner covering his loins, which depicted Ethiopia.

I noticed that I was no longer upright and that while I could still see the popcorn ceiling, I could also see it through the dark, dark brown eyes of The Moor. My heart began to pound, and the sound of it swelled through every blood vessel, culminating in my eardrum. The man from the future and present, real and dream, steadied his eyes on my eyes. *You are a manipulative coward,* the eyes said to me. *You are a taker who feigns concern to extract the essence of good and the remaining souls.*

He then placed a giant hand on my forehead. I saw myself at my job interview, then in a car talking seductively to Ruth Hightower. I saw myself engaged in conversations with dozens of Chinaberry Tree patrons, including the ones that were part of the pilgrimage of my inner circle. There was the dinner with Ethel Mann, who I convinced to put in a good word for me for a new position. The heavy hand became increasingly uncomfortable. The Moor seemed to find pleasure in pressing my head through the bed. When he slightly released his gripping palm, I saw myself at the table in The Chinaberry Tree, sitting next to Crazy Hezekiah. I saw myself straining to hear what he was saying. I felt an overwhelming flush of embarrassment at the eavesdropping. The dark, dark brown eyes returned, and I heard through sight. I knew that I would now receive what I thought I wanted to know. Crazy Hezekiah's voice started as a distant echo in a snuff box and, gradually, it became clearer, but my sense of being an intruder became nearly unbearable.

"... Then, if you can't understand the white man on your own planet, how can you possibly understand why we must do what we must do? Your world is the way it is because conquerors must always look over their backs in fear of reprisal ... You are an ant farm to us ... It's all above your head, Hezekiah ... We will only collect human DNA ... extract the propensity for violence, pride and greed ... separate out all elements of human contact with the Nephilim ... eliminate recessive genes ... remove the weeds that are choking you and your growth ... and then replant you ... We are only doing this to save you from yourselves ... Distrust abounds ... See, in a few earth years, it will become widely known that thousands of black women have been sterilized after giving birth to their first and only child ... Very soon you will know the truth behind inordinate heart problems in black boys ... You will see and reject all complex forms of escapism, from sports to game shows ... You will, in fact, see yourselves as hopeless and pathetic, and will gradually turn away from all your so-called earth religions ..."

I awakened at 3:37 a.m. The Moor said he would allow me to leave the sleep realm, but I would return to "prove" myself.

A full week had passed before Ruth picked up the jacket on her next visit to The Chinaberry Tree. Later, at home, she played back a part of the tape to determine if anything was worth saving.

"What in the hell is that?"

"That's Crazy Hezekiah," she said. "He's that weird guy who comes into The Chinaberry Tree in Ebonia at least once a month. "Oh, you know him. You've had enough drinks there, so you've probably run across him at some point. I'm gonna erase this mess."

"Wait! I'm writing a lot of stuff about Ebonia," I said. "I want to see if I can figure out what this guy is saying. Maybe it's something worthwhile." I didn't dare tell her about my dream and The Moor.

"Suit yourself," commented Ruth. "But I'm telling you, it's all gibberish."

"You're probably right," I acknowledged. "I just want to check. But that's for later. Now it's beautiful brown booty time."

Another week or so later, I transcribed the tape with Crazy Hezekiah's first set of rants and ramblings.

"I had to do a lot of work to find out what his words were," I told Ruth. "It actually made sense, like he was telling a story or something about Ebonia. Some of what he was saying could be said to be prophetic."

Ruth began reading the transcription of Crazy Hezekiah in the privacy of her bedroom one Saturday night. As she read, she said she tried to envision Crazy Hezekiah. She began to see his lips moving, and his eyes began to linger on hers as his ramblings came alive, as though he was sitting on the bed beside her.

"All in all," Crazy Hezekiah began, "most living rooms were the same. Miz Bessie Wainwright had a lamp with a small portrait of Jesus and his European disciples on its side, but so did her neighbor Miz Callie, and so did Miz Toot. Their coffee tables had all been purchased from the same Jewish vendor on Ninth Street, and their toss pillows had the same velvety texture of an era that seemed out of place. The living rooms beamed with futile attempts to portray the ambience of some cavalier nouveau riche caste …

"But the tired, obvious reality was a dingy, almost tropical cove carved out of the slave quarters of the early 1960s." Ruth paused from her reading, reasoning that he was referring to an Ebonia of decades ago. She read on, and his voice filled her ears again.

"Dusty children pelted the alleys like bewildered raindrops sent to wash away all, but instead finding nothing. Disillusioned, the rain splatters about the road, the homes, the whole community of Ebonia, its tiny droplets a million pineapples stretched out across the plain.

"The little feet of children dig into the earth as they run down the dirt roads, heaving into the soil with a surprising fierceness. The earth catapults behind their backs, launched toward oblivion. Sticky red juice shines on their necks and shoulders as they race discarded car tires down to the end of the road.

"The children run, faster and faster," Crazy Hezekiah, babbled on. "Their hands were a cyclic blur that stroked the rubber toward the Promised Land. Their feet hit the hot street like Bull Connor's stick against the nape of an unsuspecting, too-proud Negro. The winner takes all.

"Meanwhile, the parents cursed the dust of the afternoon. Some took their hoses to water down the dirt. Later, they tell their children how very fortunate they are: To be able to run and play; to have fresh souse meat in the refrigerator; and to have a chance to go to the colored school without having to worry about working the farm.

"On Sundays, they prayed hard. On Mondays, they prayed harder. Throughout the other days, they simply tried to survive, to hang on, and to avoid any of the myriad pitfalls that would make white folks mad, and to teach their children their proper place at the end of the road.

"And so, that in a nutshell is the story of the minority community of Ebonia," Crazy Hezekiah's soliloquy was coming to an end. "It is, for good or bad, a model of our place in the world. Senseless materialism, aimless ambition, and wanton assimilation—all for the sake of accommodating a doomed majority that will never accept us. Poor Ebonia. Poor me."

One day, in the parking lot, following her weekly visit to The Chinaberry Tree, Ruth asked the charming old Ethel about the story behind Crazy Hezekiah.

"I vaguely remember that the word at the time was that he was the one who set Old Man Schaumburg's house afire," Ethel had struggled to pick her own brain. "They said he sneaked back into the basement to look at some of the papers and knocked over an oil lamp. No one knows for sure, but they point to that incident as the point in time when Hezekiah went crazy. You know how folks talk, though." Ruth thought she had wasted something on her blouse, as she noticed the old woman staring in the direction of her cleavage.

"They also said that Hezekiah probably had just seen some strange writings and pictures among Schaumburg's stuff when he knocked over the oil lamp," added Ethel, raising her eyes to meet Ruth's. "But people talked about Schaumburg's being crazy, too. Said he was able to see the future and stuff like that. *Those* kind of people are the ones that scare me, honey."

Chapter 12 – Mr. Lewis' Tale

Bennie Lewis knew the hardships schools like Ebonia College had to endure over the decades. He had been there, and he had witnessed that turbulence in his own life. It was a host of memories, mostly fond ones, that spurred him to hand over to the school nearly 700 acres of sought-after land.

Born in a small village in rural Barbour County on November 29, 1933, Mr. Lewis set out for Ebonia via a short train trip from tiny Peapick, Alabama, in 1949, with only $6 in his pockets.

"This was one of the few times that coloreds, as we were called, sat in the first car of the train. This was only so that we would filter the smoke with our faces and clothes first," he remembered. "When the locomotive came close to edging through PlumNearly, about the only almost all-white community in the Black Belt, the crew had to pull down the shades so that the rednecks wouldn't know which car the coloreds were riding in. They were known to act a fool."

"Because the school session at Ebonia hadn't started," he said, "I worked the campus farm in the meantime, plowing and harvesting corn and other vegetables. I was also a custodian. See, that was during a time when industrial education was the thing."

When the session started a few weeks later, he began his studies in teacher education, all the while plowing on the farm until sunset and mopping floors in the early mornings. When the session started, he studied history, chemistry, language, biology and art with about 66 other students, he recollected.

"The campus was in terrible condition," commented Lewis. "Marcus Garvey Hall was the only brick building for men. We ate family-style in the Dining Hall. Those were the good old days. Dr. Hamilton Savery was president back then and by the time I was about to complete my studies, I was working as a student assistant in Dr. Savery's office."

Lewis told me he recalled President Savery as an approachable, "fatherly" figure, but the memory didn't bring a smile. "The school really grew under his administration, and students had a lot of respect for him," stated the retiree.

But there was a Savery that no one knew except Mr. Lewis, who was a young man around 21 when, while young Lewis was sitting at a reception desk—hiding a ham sandwich—in Dr. Savery's outer office, the president summoned him to his office.

"I need to talk to you," he said, closing the door behind them.

"Yes, sir," answered Bennie, beginning to wonder if he had done something wrong or had forgotten to deliver something across campus.

"How do you like Ebonia, Bennie?" asked President Savery, pacing behind his desk.

"I like it very much, sir." Bennie was beginning to get a little nervous. He had no idea where this conversation was going.

"Do you remember when you first came here as a scared sixteen-year-old?" queried Savery, slow and deliberate.

"Yes," said Bennie. "You pulled me to the side and told me that everything was going to be okay, to just find something to keep myself busy, and I would be looked after just fine."

"That's right," commented Savery, pleased that they were both on the same page. "I'd like to think that I kept my promise to you. Have I?"

"Oh, yes! Absolutely, sir!"

"You are almost at the end of your studies, are you not?" President Savery pulled his chair out to sit down.

"Yes, I am."

"Do you have plans for what you're going to do when you leave here?"

"I've been in contact with a cousin of mine," he stammered. "She's a teacher up near Tuscaloosa. She's gonna try to put in a good word for me there."

"Uh-huh," said President Savery, obviously unimpressed. "I have a friend in Phenix City, Noah, who's looking for someone special for a position. With a good word from me, the job could be yours. Interested?"

"Yes, sir!" Bennie was on the edge of his seat. This was a dream come true. The people back in Peapick would be able to see that he was making something of himself.

"It's not just about the job, though, Bennie," added Savery in a somber manner. "This job is part of a fellowship, a secret community of men. Once you're in, there's no limit to what you can achieve."

"What do you mean?"

"I mean," he began, clearing his throat and searching for the right words. "There's a price for the ticket."

Bennie's heart began to race. Back on the farm in Peapick, he had heard the old folks talk about 'funny men' and 'funny women.' They detested these kinds of folks because they were both scary and demonic. All of his life he had been taught that demons were inside of these kind of people and it forced them to do vile things with their bodies.

"Price?" Bennie asked. He was becoming so nervous, he thought he'd pass out.

"You haven't had a girl yet have you, Bennie?" President Savery's voice took on the tone of a smooth prosecutor.

"N-no, sir," stuttered Bennie. "That's not allowed at Ebonia."

"But you do think about young ladies, don't you?"

"Yes, sir—No, sir!" Bennie was feeling trapped. He didn't know where President Savery was going, and the old Peapick tales about demons were causing his mind havoc.

"Relax," coaxed Savery, slithering slowly in his sturdy seat situated on the side of his desk. "No one's here. You aren't in trouble or anything like that. Let's start again. You are a young man, right?"

"Yes, sir," responded Bennie, beginning to perspire and wondering why no one was entering the usually busy office.

"And you have what young men have, right?"

"Y-yes, sir," Bennie stammered.

"Okay," wrapped up Savery. "Maybe now we're getting somewhere. You do think about women don't you?"

"Yes, sir," admitted Bennie, holding his head down.

"Okay, then," triumphed President Savery. "That's great! There's nothing to be shamed of there."

Bennie let out a sigh of release. It wasn't about what he was thinking, after all. Perhaps Savery wanted to set him up with a friend's daughter. He was just making sure that the little farm boy from Peapick wasn't a funny man with demons in *his* body. Surely he could pass this test. Every morning before sunrise, he was hard as a rock, and he would have liked nothing better than to have shared this wonder with a willing female on the other side of campus. So, that's what this was all about. Maybe President Savery was just making sure he hadn't picked up some nasty woman's disease or something.

"Well," Savery went on. "Since you say you've never had a woman before, I have a proposition for you."

Bennie was becoming excited with anticipation. After getting the job, he'd probably be introduced to President Savery's friend's daughter. They'd go out on a date, get to know one another, and probably hit it right off.

"I want you to love me like I was that woman," Savery said. He paused and rested his eyes on Bennie. The sun stopped. Joshua had commanded his heart to quit beating, yet his blood continued running through his veins. The moon caused waves of confusion in Bennie, as this man he always had respected called him into a final test. And, like the lunar body outside, his stomach seemed halted on tin suspensions.

Bennie's mouth dropped.

"I'll show you all there is to know," Savery went on. "This is nothing you have to worry about anybody knowing. If this works out...well, as I told you; there's no limit to where you can go. Of course, if you say no, things will be different, because you were trusted with some information that could change you for the worst."

Bennie sat silently, almost on the brink of tears and rage.

"There's nothing back in Peapick," Savery said. "And, I know your cousin who lives outside of Tuscaloosa. There's nothing open in the school system for coloreds right now. Think on it for a few days and talk to me again when everyone has gone. I believe you'll make the right decision."

Mr. Lewis left Ebonia for his first job in Phenix City, where he was paired with President Savery's friend, Arthur Livingston. He served several years, and received numerous awards. Livingston arranged a job for him in Scottsboro through Hardy Means. Means made Bennie his personal assistant and taught him the ropes of operating within a segregated school system.

Contacting a friend in Indiana, Means sent Bennie out of the South to work on advanced degrees at Purdue. When he graduated, he returned to Ebonia, where he served as principal and later superintendent of schools. He re-established his relationship with a much older President Savery. This time, Savery became a true father figure. Savery and his wife had no children, and she preceded him in death. When he died a few years later, he willed a lot of land to Mr. Lewis and a few of his friends that were in what he referred to as "The Inner Circle."

"For what it's worth," Mr. Lewis once said one afternoon on his ranch, "I wouldn't take anything for the experiences I've had. I know I'm simply part of a continuum. My experiences came as they did, because others had experiences that greatly impacted their lives, as well.

"We all have a soul," said Mr. Lewis, a man who now was known for the way he worked with spirits. "Even those people with demons wrecking their bodies."

Chapter 13 – Franklin's Tale

Franklin was the archivist at Ebonia College. His specialty was the life of Dr. Hamilton Savery. He had talked with scores of old citizens, had visited the home of the Savery family near the Mississippi River, and had meticulously studied the former President's papers. Franklin rarely talked to the other clients at The Chinaberry Tree, unless the subject somehow centered on Ebonia College's past or the Savery Administration.

According to Franklin, Dr. Hamilton Savery grew up in western Mississippi, where he and his friend Jeremiah played cowboys and Indians in the thick woods and tried to dodge an evil white farmer named Hopewell. Hopewell had a thing for black boys.

Hamilton had a lot of privileges growing up, even though he was a black child in Mississippi. His smooth brown skin and wavy hair exhibited his family's Indian connection, and his father had mastered a way to hold on to his land for a decent living. Jeremiah's folks hadn't been so lucky. They were now working for Hopewell on land that used to be theirs. His father was struggling to make ends meet tilling Hopewell's farm, while his mother supplemented their livelihood with her expertise in voodoo. Jeremiah no longer had as much time to play.

On the few occasions the 12-year-olds would get together, Jeremiah acted troubled. He wouldn't want to play, and he'd hardly talk.

"What's the matter with you?" asked Hamilton one summer day, as they sat in a field on the Saverys' farm.

"Nothing," replied Jeremiah, staring off into space.

"Well, how come you don't want to play anymore?" Hamilton asked. He wanted to run widely into the field, to climb a small tree's top limb and ride it down to the ground like a wild pony.

"If I tell you something, will you promise not to tell anyone else," Jeremiah had asked him.

"I won't tell," young Hamilton promised. "What's it about? Is it about your folks?"

"No," said Jeremiah half-heartedly, drawing a ring in the dirt.

"What then?"

"It's 'bout Hopewell," he said, still looking down at the ground.

"What about him?" Hamilton sat on the ground next to him.

"He nasty." Jeremiah slowly looked up so that Hamilton's eyes met his.

"I know that," Hamilton said, laughingly. "Everybody knows he's nasty and he stinks."

"Dat ain't what I's sayin'," continued Jeremiah. "He made me hold him in ma mouth." Jeremiah started to cry. Hamilton's heart paused for the first time. A long silence followed.

"Your daddy knows?"

"No."

"Mama?"

"No," he repeated. "Just my older sister."

"I'm telling my daddy!" Hamilton rose up. "My daddy can't stand those peckawoods! He can't do that to you."

"Ham, I told you not to tell anybody!" shouted Jeremiah, starting to cry again. "I don't want dem to know!"

Hamilton, fueled by years of having his way because he was a cute child of means for his day, had gone too far to turn back. He sympathized with Jeremiah and all, but that Hopewell son of a bitch had better start to hoping.

Hamilton waited until his father was relaxing with his pipe following supper, his right hand stuffed in his overalls, tilted back on a straw bottom chair on the front porch. His father listened intently, then his nostrils flared. He went and got his shotgun, hitched up the mule and headed up the road a piece to talk with Jeremiah's father. Within ten minutes both men were taking the mules over to Hopewell's. Once there, they shot his dogs and damn near shot him. His wife ranted on about how they had always got along with the coloreds.

"No Klan in these parts, Hopewell," Hamilton's father said.

"I got a good mind to make one of ya put *me* in yo' mouth," screamed Jeremiah's daddy.

"Look here, boy," negotiated Hopewell. "We don't want no trouble here. Ain't no harm done. I was jes playin' with him. I'd just peed, that's all. I was playin' with him; didn't mean for his mouth to touch it!"

Several times after the incident, Hamilton would enter Hopewell's property and wait until he saw Hopewell somewhere in the yard. He didn't have to fear Hopewell's dogs any longer. He'd yell from a distance: "I was jes playin'!" Then he would run back between the trees to the farm.

One day Hamilton wasn't so lucky. So used to being treated with respect and with favor, Hopewell caught and slapped the boy. Hopewell placed his vice grip hands around Hamilton's neck, took out his white member and forced Hamilton's head to his groin. Later, he wiped the boy's face with his shirt and told him to take his "sorry ass" home.

Hamilton was devastated and humiliated. He spat all the way home. He said nothing to his father about the incident.

A week later, however, he opened up to Jeremiah, who still walked around in a daze.

"I think I know how you feel, Jeremiah," said Hamilton.

"You mean he—"

"Uh-huh." Hamilton did not beg for Jeremiah's silence, and Jeremiah did not promise it. When their two fathers had a chance to come before the peckawood again, Hopewell and his filthy crew were packing to move to Scott, Mississippi. Hopewell's wife was expecting a child. Jeremiah's mama placed a curse on the baby, and she said their crops and land would be swallowed up by a large flood.

Hamilton seemingly recuperated from the incident, and he built a small circle of close, but violated, friends to carry him through it. Jeremiah, however, developed a series of emotional problems throughout the rest of his life.

A year after Hopewell had moved near Greenville, in 1927, a series of levees began to give way from parts of Missouri, Arkansas and further South.

Hopewell's farmland in Scott was buried under several feet of water, and people sat on their rooftops, waiting to be rescued. Unable to swim, his frail wife was frantic. When help finally arrived, she missed a step as she was getting on the small boat. She fell into the water, taking the newborn with her. She panicked so much that the baby kept plunging underneath her thrusts into the muddy water. She flapped wildly to save herself, and Hopewell had jumped in to calm her, but she was too frightened. Oddly, no one attempted to help them. He finally calmed her enough to take her back to the boat, where a lone black boy offered his hand to pull them aboard. The boy later managed to recover the infant, but it was no longer breathing.

Chapter 14 – Peter's Tale

It had been several years since Peter had last visited his folks on Ebonia's Spring Street. Thank God for his brother Paul. Had not the latter been such a staunch believer in the family, Peter would have succumbed to the days and weeks that so easily claim years from people.

Over a few drinks at The Chinaberry Tree one evening, Peter and I talked about one of his rare trips home to Ebonia. Paul always got on him about his lack of concern for the kinfolks.

"It's going on three years, Peter," Paul said to Peter on Easter Sunday. "You didn't make Thanksgiving. You didn't make Christmas–what's wrong with you? Don't you believe in family?"

Paul always aligned his supporting statements in such a way that his final points of persuasion—*Don't you realize we're brothers? Of course you know Papa isn't getting any younger, don't you? Don't you believe in family?*—were overkill.

Somewhere along the line, Peter had lost his place as the prospective rock of the family. It didn't matter. With Paul, the family was still in capable hands. Nonetheless, Paul lacked Peter's sensitivity, his annoying eye for detail. Yet, whenever Peter thought he could win certain favor from their Mama and Papa by zigging, Paul would zag and steal the show.

"No sweet potatoes for me, Mama," Peter said during Christmas four years ago. He was a gainfully employed bachelor and wanted his Mama to be impressed that he was watching his intake. "I've been working out ... trying to keep the weight down."

Mama seemed to take it all in stride, even managed a slight smile. He could tell she really liked this holiday scene. Papa sat to the west of the common, stick-leg kitchen table, never missing the left table leg with his large feet. When Paul and Peter were kids, Papa often knocked over mason jars of Kool-aid, because even then he misjudged that same table leg. Mama sat opposite Papa, on the east end of the kitchen table. Paul usually sat on the north side of the table, with his back to cupboard, while Peter sat on the south side of the table with his back to the stove.

They didn't do the passing bit. Before sitting down, Mama always fixed the plates for her men, starting with

Papa. Peter was next, because he was the oldest of the two. It was a special place, especially since she would no doubt feel all warm inside, knowing that he was being responsible and mature about what he ate. Then it was Paul's turn.

"Sweet potatoes?" Mama asked Paul. She wore her favorite tent-style brown dress, and her hair was pulled back in a bun. Although she didn't have one wrinkle, her true age was beginning to catch up to her face.

"I'll take Peter's," Paul said. Mama laughed as though everything she had ever done for them had now found appreciation. Throughout the meal, Peter gnawed on the knowledge that he was no longer the favorite son.

Of course, going so far off to college for a major in psychology hadn't helped him. Paul stayed within the state and dashed home a lot on weekends. He kept his fingers on the pulse of change on Spring Street, which had become Ebonia's wasteland. Only a handful of whites remained in Ebonia, but there remained a slave mentality. Unlike Papa and Peter, Paul did not allow Spring Street to bother him. It took a while for Papa to convert the Spring Street that fathered him into a place where he could raise family and a community. Paul grew up through Papa's gradual transformation. Primarily owing to the infrequent trips home, Peter still saw a Papa of more than twenty years ago.

Now, he was driving home again, at the urging of Paul. Speeding southbound on Interstate 65, he began to wrestle with why going home was such an ordeal for him. The cornfields of southern Indiana raced by.

Spring Street had always been "home" for Papa and Peter, protecting boyhoods, if such security can be borne of rows upon rows of shotgun houses, built on uneven bricks and hoisted some three feet above the ground. Paul was more a man of the world, the type who could pitch a tent on any terrain. That was the only chasm that separated the men at 7 Spring Street. Paul rode Spring Street like the Natchez hooker it was, but Spring Street rode Papa and Peter.

To the outsider, the street wasn't much for the eyes. It was, in retrospect, Alabama's version of a South African shantytown. Dusty black children for decades had stomped down every blade of grass around each and every rectangular box villagers called home. As a matter of fact, it never was really a "street" in the truest sense of the word. It was by and large unwanted, unpaved and unattended. Nonetheless, what set Spring Street apart from the others on the west side of the railroad tracks was that it was also inexplicably unaware.

A criminal before a hostile courtroom, Spring Street was a place without memory or recall. Although everyone was poor, no one knew just why. Most people who lived there were happy, and had been happy even for as long as Papa could remember. Every day, mamas and daddies used the lion's share of their lives securing the mundane. Too many years were wasted in providing for shoes, fixing hopeless cars, and keeping the lights on in dark, single-barrel houses. *If we work hard, the Lord will bless us—somehow,* they would say. And, I guess, in a way He *did.* They had been blessed, it would seem, with no memory. Any allusion to the Motherland or their proud African heritage had been erased by time. They had been cruelly forced into the role of lost Israel and were playing to an empty theatre.

There were no memories or tales of a great and powerful Egypt. The sun rose and set on the pyramids formed by their A-frame roofs, not on a land of kings and queens. For the residents of Spring Street, the past was lodged in the bowels of red Alabama clay or in the cotton fields of east Mississippi. They had heard nothing of the Ivory Coast or Ghana or Senegal. They were forgotten children prodded to sing old songs in a new land, and the total worth of their souls had been paid for with a heaping spoonful of amnesia.

Without true memories, they could be happy in neighborhood kennels, in the concentration camps for Negroes that dotted the American South. They could drive by mansions built with their labor, work at places through which they entered via back doors, and accept bones as full-course meals. If it's true what the old folks used to say about God—that he works through people—then Spring Street's only ram in the bush at the time was Mr. Upchurch.

Like the neighborhood street on which he lived, Mr. Upchurch wasn't much for the eyes. He had a long, bullet-shaped head, a neck that seemed a little too short for the load it had to carry, and a butt that was perhaps a tad bit too large for even a black man. Word had it that with hellfire Mr. Upchurch had cursed his white boss at the foundry over in Saxonville. Before people could pity him and ask what he planned to do to support his family, he had opened up the front part of his house as a neighborhood store. Since no one gave two damns about what happened on Spring Street, he had managed to purchase a business license without a single query about zoning restrictions. Imagine that: a business license to operate a store in a shotgun house in a shot-down neighborhood filled with shot-down dreams. It was a street only an insurance peddler could love.

Sometimes Peter would run down the street with a nickel in hand, anxious to spend it at Mr. Upchurch's store on a Big Time candy bar. Fatherly, he would place his hand on his head.

"Peter!" he would exclaim during the anointing. "I kin look at yo fo'head and tell you want a Big Time!"

"Yessuh!"

"Want some of dat choc'lit and peanuts and caramel, don't you?"

"Yessuh!" chimed Peter, jumping up and down, as the old hand tried to steady him. Something about Mr. Upchurch's hand on him made him feel complete.

"Well, listen heah. You don't think white folks gone let colored boys like you have a Big Time for a nickel, do you? They won't even want you to have a *little* time for a nickel."

"Ain't no white folks 'round here, Mr. Upchurch," he said. Theatrically, the store owner looked around him, chuckled to himself and then aloud. "I guess you's right, Peter. I guess you's right." He handed over the candy bar and took the nickel.

"But ... I'm gonna put a foot in your butt if you don't come in heah wid a dime next time. Big Time's a dime, son!" he laughed as Peter ran toward home. "Big Time's a dime!"

During summer weekends, Papa liked to walk down the alley to Mr. Upchurch's place for a game of checkers on the front porch. Papa was an unassuming man, a sparrow among many. He was usually quiet except for the occasional late night murmurings in the middle passage. On Peter's cot in the front room, he would hear the innocuous discussion between a quiet man and a usually domineering woman become transformed, with Papa demanding between the headboard's assaults on the walls, "Who's da man?"

One thing that set Papa apart from other men on Spring Street—even apart from Mr. Upchurch—was his reflective demeanor. When he was sitting among a group of people, everyone wanted to know what he was thinking. They could rest easier, somehow, if he would simply let it out, no matter what it was. He garnered a respect on Spring Street, if not admiration.

He was a good man. He brought home his pay, didn't smoke filterless Camels, drink gin or chase women. That's what Grandma told Mama whenever Mama said she couldn't understand Papa. Sometimes, Paul and Peter couldn't understand their Papa, either. The angrier he got, the more he would use words and paint pictures that scared them. At other times, he seemed that he was right on the edge, mired in a bitterness so deep that his family was too helpless to retrieve him.

Whenever he would wrestle a game away from Mr. Upchurch, Papa returned from his inner cliffs and proclaimed, "Who's da man?" Peter and Paul simply watched and smiled, thinking it was just another adult thing. But they could sometimes hear Miss Lizzie, who lived in the shotgun house next to them, laughing. They played a few more rounds and carried on as if they were the best of friends. Then Mr. Upchurch invited Papa to come to Sunday worship services with him sometime, and Papa's smile disappeared. He quickly grabbed his hat to leave. At that point, it was Mr. Upchurch's turn.

"Who's da man?" he yelled, taunting Papa, who rushed off up the alley. "Who's da man? Jesus! Who's da man? Jesus!" Papa picked up the pace as though the Devil had poked him with a hot fork and asked for dark meat.

Louisville. Home of Cassius Clay.

It was during those lazy summer days that Papa, Mr. Upchurch and all of Spring Street were "eating high on the hog," as Mama would put it. It was the best of times, in the worst of places.

On some days, Mr. Upchurch gathered the children around the front porch of the store and read stories for what seemed like forever. They didn't mind the heat, and the parents—especially if he kept them captivated for at least an hour or two—were happy for the moments alone. One day, when Peter was picking up some plain flour for Mama, Miss Gertrude came in the store with her new baby. She didn't see Peter because he was a little shorter than the single row of merchandise positioned in the middle of the store.

"You know you need to lay off them damn stories," she said to Mr. Upchurch. "I don't know what you men folks done conjured up, but ain't a woman on the street can keep her dress down when you start that storytellin'. This'n here is yourns," she said, laughing, holding the baby out, as if offering it to Mr. Upchurch.

"Shoot," he said, bearing a wide, beautiful smile, decked in overalls too neat for the surroundings. "Get on outta heah wid that foolishness! Anyway, dontcha see there's a child in heah, woman?" He pointed Peter out to her as he stepped away from the mound, as if on cue.

"Who?" She followed his finger to the end of the partition, where Peter stood with a two-pound bag of flour with a face towel attached. "Oh," she said, in a dry monotone. "It's little 'Who's da Man?'" For a moment there was a nervous silence. Then, with thunder, the two of them laughed so hard Peter thought the floor would never stop shaking. Thinking back over all those years, Peter told me his Papa would have died if he knew his bedroom antics were common fodder on Spring Street.

Mr. Upchurch had a way of bringing out the best in everybody, without really trying. Miss Gertrude was usually a little on the mean side. But Mr. Upchurch made her laugh. Old nosy Miss Lizzie, who "felt on" young boys if left alone with them too long, acted quite dignified around Mr. Upchurch. Even usually fly-on-the-wall Papa was like Paul Roberson whenever shoulder to shoulder with Mr. Upchurch. It seemed that no one had a cross to bear that Mr. Upchurch could not help them carry. Although he was only seven years older than Papa, Mr. Upchurch was the chief of the village.

The few kids who had earlier managed to escape shantytown for a college education found it imperative to report to Mr. Upchurch about their progress and experiences. For the church a few blocks away, he was a loyal trustee. For Mrs. Upchurch and his two daughters, he was a personification of the Lord.

Later, when Peter was about twelve, the brothers still found enjoyment in the Papa/Mr. Upchurch competition one day in early June. He noticed that Mr. Upchurch had begun to lose some weight and looked much better. Everyone was noticing and complimenting him on his new look. He had even talked Papa into going to "the House of the Lord." A telephone call from Aunt Martha sent Paul and Peter packing for a summer in St. Louis. Too young to know they were simply trading slums, the boys thought the river town was like the Promised Land. They had a ball, met new friends, maneuvered big city life and, even though not quite teens, got lucky.

Many times Papa was down the alley visiting Mr. Upchurch when Mama called them during the summer. Papa even managed the store, while Mr. Upchurch had to go away for a week, Mama said. It seemed all was well at home in Alabama. That was all Paul and Peter needed to hear. More fun and play. More summer in St. Louis.

The summer came to an abrupt end. By the time they returned in late August, Spring Street had become a foreign country. The news hit like a 1964 Chevy: Mr. Upchurch was dying. Even the lingering joys of St. Louis could not prepare them for the suffering that became embedded in their psyches. Almost every night, they listened to Mr. Upchurch moan in agony.

"Let's go down to the store," Paul coaxed Peter one day in early September.

"No, I don't want to go down there." He knew he would not be able to take seeing another Mr. Upchurch, one different from the one he had grown to love and admire. Paul, though younger, was tougher—or dumber. With him, sometimes the two were synonymous. In October, even Mama tried to get him to walk down the street with her to visit him. Papa only asked Peter once, back in August, and said he understood. He had been asked three times and by three of the people he loved most in the world, but he did not bulge. The evenings in their narrow home had become somber. And, for all the nights Peter could not sleep, there was hardly a stir in the middle passage, either.

Sure, Papa had started going to church in the summer. But by the time December came, possessed by his first drunken stupor, Papa cursed the Lord out like no sailor could ever do. Paul, who slept on a cot in the kitchen, ran through Mama and Papa's room to the front room to join Peter. Paul, The Builder, was falling apart!

Papa asked the Lord squarely what his plans were for the Black man in America. He wanted to know if the Lord was misleading him, using him for the white man.

"How in the hell can a *chosen* people put up with this bullshit?" screamed Papa. Mama tried to calm him. The boys sat frozen on Peter's cot. This wasn't Papa. "Four hundred years of crap in this damn Egypt! Goddamn it! I *know* the Red Sea is really the Atlantic Ocean! These damn Africans you got stranded on this alley might not know any better, but I know!"

Now they *knew* this wasn't Papa. Papa talking geography? He couldn't even spell Atlantic—could he? They talked about the Atlantic in school. Parents just didn't talk school talk at home. Where was he getting all of this stuff?

"Moses, you're getting yourself all worked up," they heard Mama say to him. They knew their parents were probably sitting on the edge of their bed. "Don't talk to the Lord like that. Calm down, baby."

Papa wept. "Mary?"

"Yes, baby?" answered Mama.

"Why would any poor-ass nigger living in this god-forsaken land believe in his enemy's god?"

"Moses! Stop that! You stop that kinda talk right now! No one owns God, baby. God isn't used; He uses. Don't disown God. Nobody down here looks more like they were made from the earth than us. Look, I know things have been tough. You had a good thing going in college and then I up and got pregnant. It changed things, and not for the better. But we have to hang in there, baby. We've got to reach our dreams through our children. Things have got to be better."

"Mary, don't you see it?" asked Papa, and Paul and Peter could hear the tears and deep hurt in his voice. "Things aren't going to get better for us. Did it get better for Upchurch? Black folks are dropping like flies of cancer and white man diseases all over this damned place! It's no accident. This is *not* our ship. This is *not* our country. We are out of sync here."

"We are not the ones out of place, Moses! This here's *our* world! It's all we know," Mama said. "It's all we have."

"You deserve more, Mary."

"You have three people who love you and a God who's simply waiting on you," they heard Mama tell Papa. "The Lord put color in most of the people in the world, so he likes variety. Paint Him any way you want to, but love Him. Maybe history has scraped the paint off of Him—I really don't know. I do know He's the best weapon you have for the war you're fighting."

Silence followed for a long time. The train coupled a quarter-mile up the road. Then, the quiet became a little eerie. Paul began to snore. Softly, ever so faintly, Peter heard the headboard brush against the wall in the Motherland. He knew that, at least for tonight, all would be all right. As he stared at the ceiling from his cot, he tried to understand what was troubling Papa. He couldn't.

Nashville. Country Music Capital of the World.

Before Thanksgiving and throughout much of December, people on Spring Street felt the cruel winter of Mr. Upchurch's delicate existence. Those brave souls who made constant vigils to his bedside reported a man literally ravaged by colon cancer. It was unbearable for everyone. Even worse, they began to wonder whether their prayers were being—had *ever* been—heard.

"Oh, Jesus! Jesus! *Take me!*" Mr. Upchurch's groans got louder and more constant in December. His pleas went on for hours and hours. Eventually, Mama, Paul and

Peter learned to sleep through it. So did most of the other people on Spring Street, but only after hating him first. He had been the hope of the community and a heaven in health. But now that he was taking them through his hell, they were forced to deal with the fact that hope could only come from on high. And, they couldn't place it on the tab. He forced them to realize that there could be another side to unanswered prayers, that there could be futility in a life devoted to service and good. If it could happen to a man like Mr. Upchurch, what hope did anyone else have? Were they simply kidding themselves? Papa was a little blunter about it. Sometimes Paul and Peter were awakened by Papa's screaming, not Mr. Upchurch's. "Why doesn't the Lord take him, goddamit?!" Papa would shout, almost at the top of his lungs. On Christmas, Papa got up in a good mood. He said he had the best sleep he had had in a long time. While they were eating breakfast, Miss Lizzie called and said Mr. Upchurch had died around 3:37 a.m.

Birmingham. The Magic City.

But that was many years ago. Even now, as Peter drives the last thirty-three miles home, *that* Spring Street will no doubt seem a winter-cold and faraway place. There's no Mr. Upchurch to share old college tales or experiences from Chicago. Paul would arrive in a day or so, anxious to tell him about the girls he has mounted at Tuskegee. He hoped Mama was baking some macaroni and cheese, fixing a mess of collards with a big piece of ham hock. He even wanted a large heaping of sweet potatoes, too.

Almost there.

The shotgun houses have given way to slick, too-neat prefabricated homes. They aren't mansions, but they are certainly a step in the right direction. He drives slowly, out of old habit, across once-bumpy railroad tracks toward the new pyramids of a not-so-old Egypt. He turns on the newly paved road. As he almost coasts along Spring Street, he sees a flock of kids sitting Indian-style on fresh, green, green grass and around the front porch of ... yes—it's his house! They are all laughing hysterically.

A recent custom during the summers, Papa has run some water from the hose to form a puddle at the curb, so that the sparrows could have water to drink. They walk on the water as the fire from the hot paved street rises behind them. Mama, perhaps, has pushed a dozen or so overflowing flowerpots to one side of the porch, out of the way of the children, yet forming a large bouquet more beautiful than anything she could have ever intended to make.

He sees Papa sitting on a wicker-bottom chair among the children. He pulls up along the curb, parks, gets out, and stands alongside his car.

"Hello! Welcome home, Peter ... son," said Papa, looking up from his captive audience of Ebonia's future.

"Hello, Papa."

He listens, fascinated, as Papa continues to spin a tale about his youth as a prince in a faraway land. Peter's world is turned upside down. Papa is no longer a prisoner of Spring Street. He has put its cross aside. Paul had refused to carry it at all. Though he went away, Spring Street was still inside of Peter. He had refused to let it go. He realized now that he hadn't traveled so far, after all.

"*You* weren't a prince!" a little boy said, eventually, laughing.

"He could've been," said another.

Chapter 15 – Isaac's Tale

Few men in Ebonia were as fascinating as Dr. Isaac N. Speights. A long-time physicist who was likely turning 50, he had a charisma that captivated anyone with the slightest interest in scientific wonder.

A gin and tonic man, Isaac could elaborate on nearly any subject. Most of his time at The Chinaberry Tree was spent perusing those obscure journals only read by a handful of nerds. Understandably, he rarely engaged in conversations with most of the other clients. However, Isaac's true gift was in making the complicated simple. He had a God-given knack for putting hieroglyphics in layman's terms.

One typical Friday evening, while Bo Willie, Trent, Brad and Reverend Wright were hypnotically engaged in a fiery conversation about the correlation between the width and depth of a woman's butt and the temperature of her poontang, Isaac carried on a side conversation about new scientific breakthroughs.

"The great Galileo made the modern telescope what it is today," Isaac said, looking up toward the ceiling, as though he was imitating an ancient astronomer. "But that was more than four centuries ago. You'd think that someone would have come up with something a little more profound in all that time. But not much has happened to revolutionize that one little instrument yet. I mean, scientists, researchers and venture capitalists have come together to chew the fat on a few things, but the bottom line is that, where the telescope is concerned, there's still nothing new under the sun."

Isaac then went on to compare the lull in telescopic discovery with human lovemaking. "There are a lot of different ways of doing it all over the world," he said. "But the ultimate goal is to fertilize the egg. Without that happening often enough, everything else is just an exercise in futility. There are different kinds of telescopes, huge ones, small ones, expensive ones, and cheap ones. But they are all designed to help a person see something totally out of the league of the naked eye."

There are so many things that can't be seen with the naked eye, stated Isaac. He said no one in Jesus' time expected him to come as a babe in a manger in a Bethlehem stable. Likewise, people with the major influence on American life, its finances, its health and its opinions, waste most of the nation's research and development resources on the toys of people who look like them. No one will look in a Tuskegee lab for the undeniable cure for cancer, because it is common knowledge among the pillars of influence that the monies allotted for research there should not yield a difference, a difference determined by those who choose Nobels.

"But thank God that differences are often made where people fail to look," Isaac explained. "For instance, my best friend attended a national conference on imaging telescopes that wasn't at an Ivy League school or so-called flagship. Wanna know where it was held?"

Mr. Lewis, Peter and I sat in wonderment. "It was at—"

"Negroni!" shouted Mr. Butler, proudly placing his showpiece on the counter.

"It was at a *black* university," Isaac went on, though Mr. Butler had interrupted him as he presented the actual name. Peter and I glanced at one another. "That's right: at an HBCU. And, at the time, famous scientists like H. John Caulfield and Daryush Ila were running the show."

Isaac said his friend explained to him that while the telescopic capability exists to see heavenly bodies at unimaginable distances from the earth, the end result has been little more than a portrait on a canvas.

"These guys, at a predominantly black school—in Alabama—were talking about 'innovations and alternatives' to the tried and true imaging telescopes," Isaac beamed in awe. "Now someone, perhaps someone in a very insular world, might wonder: Why would these geniuses be there, of all places? And that would be a fair question. I mean, Caulfield had authored at least six books and 30 book chapters, so why would a physicist of that magnitude convene a group of the world's leading opticists, holographers and computer scientists at a black school in Alabama?"

"Bethlehem?" responded Peter.

"No doubt," said Isaac. "See, that school had the hard-won potential to produce more black Ph.D.'s in physics than any other school in the United States. Its physics-friendly campus had been blessed with millions in research dollars. It's a jewel that only a precious few know about."

Like that noted physicist at a black school in the Heart of Dixie, Isaac believed modern technology that has the power to enrich the human spirit should also leave its mark on the means we use to observe other worlds. "There's no reason we shouldn't apply these massive supercomputers, contemporary math and digital computing to generate three-dimensional images from telescopes in addition to drones and numerous other innovations," commented Isaac, motioning to Mr. Butler to switch him to beer.

Isaac's scientific repertoire was extensive, and he was apt to change topics in midstream. Ebonia's lone physicist went on to talk about the development of sensory devices to detect weaknesses in bridges, another research activity his friend discovered while visiting labs at fellow black schools.

But there were other favorite subjects, as well. For instance, Isaac pinpointed the decline of American global influence at 1957, almost immediately after it had begun. Instead of embarking upon a plan to make its citizens true Americans, it ignored its racialized, fragmented society and worked feverishly to help build the destroyed post-World War II societies of white Europe, he said.

"Although America had missed the atrocities of the Great War," Isaac said to me over ice cold beers in The Chinaberry Tree one Friday, "it failed to see the atrocities in its own backyard. Rather than try to make true Americans of the black people it had used for hundreds of years and to build up a scientific infrastructure to lift all of its citizens, it toyed with the stupid ideas of its pseudo-intellectuals, white supremacists and dykes to give credence to eugenics, forced sterilization and the manipulation of the leaders of black institutions. Just keeping it real."

He noted that Russia was left with nothing but a morsel of integrity, and it molded that into a mighty show of national pride in the creation of Sputnik. For some reason, America has been sold a bill of goods that national dysfunction can continue forever and that "the world will wait on us as we work it out." Isaac said people make a grave mistake by merely gazing over history. History has all the answers, but they have to be juxtaposed with searches for the right questions, he said, downing the remainder of his second gin.

"Those questions can't be guided with the precision of an old-ass AIM-9 Sidewinder, either," Isaac said, his eyes increasingly intense and his voice rising in excitement. "We're talking StormBreakers and hypersonics, baby."

He swigged his beer and looked out the window at a typical American small town, with the exception of its demographics. I ordered another set of beers as Isaac collected his thoughts. I knew there was more to come.

The Chinaberry Tree had the quaint feeling of an old medieval tavern. Warm wood with faux candles set on trays suspended from the ceiling with large chains. It was both intimate and expansive enough to accommodate a pilgrimage to the shrine of Saint Thomas Becket.

"Many black college campuses have buildings named for Northern philanthropists," Isaac started up again. "But another equally interesting question is 'how many Northern philanthropists also supported the eugenics movement?' We have to be extra careful of so-called science that hides agenda. We can never lose sight of the fact that we are all constantly evolving. We cannot deny any group the inherent right to evolve."

Isaac explained that a world controlled by people who view themselves as "supreme" is a world wracked by every extreme imaginable. It destroys ethical science and medicine. It detours genuine research, pushes forced sterilizations, restricts the same immigration that allowed the "supreme" into the country, and leads to institutionalization, discrimination and the diversion of leadership, said Isaac. "When all is said and done, there really aren't any great peoples at a national level," reflected Isaac. "Of course, it's a massive oversimplification, but once you extract the raids, occupations, conquests, atrocities of colonialism, the exacerbation of events like the Irish Potato Famine, the Transatlantic Slave Trade, land partitions and shit like that over the years—there's really nothing for *any* people to brag about."

With another sip, Isaac looked out the window again in a reflective gaze that seemed to take him beyond the town square and toward the A-frame houses of Spring Street.

Chapter 16 – Ray-Ray's Tale

"When Egypt was in its 24th dynasty, Europe was coming into its own with Homer's Iliad and Odyssey," grinned a matter-of-fact Ray-Ray, a self-proclaimed militant who had never fully left the 1960s. "*That's* vintage John Henrik Clarke, baby! The Nubian civilization south of Egypt had moved northward when Europe was a puking baby."

Ray-Ray quoted what the black historian claimed in the way that many people quote Jesus or the Bible. Tank, his sidekick, sat on The Chinaberry Tree's sidelines, urging him on. "Mother Africa has *always* had what Europeans wanted, were dying to have, but couldn't be trusted to pay for. You don't pay for things you own. That's why it has been so important all these years for whites to own everything. It took them centuries to learn that if you own everything, then you're responsible for everything and nothing at the same time."

To look at Ray-Ray was to look at some centuries-old painting of some hefty-built Moor, a captivating work of art that had been hidden and forgotten. At a precise moment on an Arabian-influenced path, the work of art had been revered. However, with just a quaint twist of fate, it had become too masculine, too dark, and simply too powerful to have casually hanging around. When Ray-Ray moved, even while heavily clothed, every inch of his person seemed to ride in sync. Although his traps were not hideously overdeveloped like some he-man, his chiseled head sat upon them like a boulder that had earned its place along a stretch on an interstate running through the Southwest. He walked about the bar's floor, all 250 pounds of him, his forearms swinging large hands back and forth, sanctioned by well-toned biceps and highly defined delts. His pecs and upper abs were always in competition for which muscle group contributed most to his undeniably V-shaped torso. Their contest was held oblivious to Ray-Ray's mighty lats and lower back.

Thus, even in his most loose dress pants, Ray-Ray's glutes, hams and inverted bowling pin calves were otherworldly. Throughout so many of his evenings, he was as committed to fine-tuning his body as he was to honing in on the why's of ancient black history, both almost to a fault.

Ray-Ray loved to explain the world according to what he had learned first-hand from leading African American historians. He was only surpassed in his research by Tank—only Tank could rarely get a word in when Ray-

Ray was warmed up. The historians were a constant pair. There was the nearly too-perfect Ray-Ray and the average looking Tank. No one to this day was even sure how Tank had gotten his name. Perhaps it was from his short, tank-like body. But it could have as easily been attributed to his barrel-shaped head, which reminded a discerning one of an old wringer washing machine. Sure, he had all the necessary and working parts, but that was it. And, hanging with a guy like Ray-Ray certainly didn't help.

"The Great One used to say that Europe never brought civilization to any land it touched, but only destroyed civilizations it could not understand," preached Ray-Ray, trying to coax Isaac and Mr. Lewis to join in the conversation. They wouldn't bite, so he turned to his trusted buddy Tank instead. "Clarke referred to these takeovers as the 'bastardization' of a people, and this went on from the brief control of the Greeks to the more sadistic control of the Romans. Except for the wealth of Africa, Rome would not have been able to sustain itself."

"Tell it!" shouted Tank.

What a diatribe against the displayed ignorance of black history among a half-buzzed citizenry in a black-owned bar! It was too bad that Ray-Ray did not meet with too many takers. This lackluster response made him feel a little superior in his research. But there were likely a score of reasons that The Chinaberry Tree faithful were not biting. For both Mr. Lewis and Ethel Mann, the foray into ancient days was overkill. Besides, digging too far into the past would only make the white man throw in your face a new set of tools and potions that you didn't even realize he had stolen from you. It's utter futility to expect humanity from someone whose past has proven him inhuman. These were not just the thoughts of patrons like Mr. Lewis or Isaac or Ethel, either. Many of the bar's faithful had boldly said these things straight to *my* face.

Bo Willie could have told Ray-Ray that, while keeping the past to your chest seems like the way sometimes, it could also tear you apart. *Let even the white people, like Arnold, be the heroes of their past,* he would have said. Isaac could have let Ray-Ray know that supremacy is too strong a word for anyone held in place on a dot in the universe and who only has two eyes and one head.

Still, Ethel—and even Crazy Hezekiah—could have told him that one shouldn't have to go too far back to prove blacks as the Chosen People. There's a reason, she said once over her drink from an oval window, that blacks are scrubbed out of ancient history. She refused, however, to share it and told patrons in earshot to find it for themselves. She did add that the story of blacks in the U.S. alone is enough proof that they are The Chosen. Throughout all the darkness, they are constantly pulling out light, which makes them images of God. From despair, they pulled forth the blues, jazz, spirituals, R&B and more. Give them opportunities, then they will shine and make others question the history books, the books that dared to exclude them! What fools want to be reminded of their hatred and mistreatment of The Chosen Ones?

Those present sat in relative silence, though.

"Anyway, Roman rule recognized the skill of African intellectuals and ascribed to them high administrative posts as emperors and popes without color prejudice. However, Roman taxation and oppression caused these severely oppressed people to consider new gods. They pulled from African folklore the account of a child who would come to deliver them," taught Ray-Ray.

He said that it was this religious concept out of African roots that was given a European face under Constantine with the aid of the Nicene Conference. This marked the European concept of Christianity and commissioned propaganda, he claimed.

According to Dr. Ray-Ray, Africans and Arabs both conquered and embellished Spain, and they drove Europe out of the Mediterranean. "It was the loss of access to African wealth that pushed Europe into the Dark Ages. Africa, on the other hand, was enjoying its Third Golden Age."

"What brought Europe back on the map?" he asked. "Do you know, Ethel? Of course not!"

"Hey!" responded Ethel immediately. "Don't play me short, young buck. It was the sale of human beings from Africa that revitalized Europe and later helped to build America. That, too, is vintage John Henrik Clarke, young fella. Since Africans were considered 'outside of God's grace,' Spain and Portugal were granted permission from the Pope to carve up Africa and to enslave its people. Throughout, the Zulu and Shanti nations fought hard. The Christian nation of England entered the slave trade with a vengeance, and, by the 19th Century, the concept of slavery yielded to colonialism in Africa. Later, the Berlin Conference of 1885 offered other European nations a ticket to the African banquet."

"Say it, my proud African queen!" exclaimed a jubilant Tank.

Ray-Ray looked stunned. It was rare that others would actually carve out a piece of his soapbox for themselves. "Very good, Ethel."

Ethel also reminded the young buck that history is filled with as much bullshit as the people who lived it.

But it was the Civil Rights Era that was Ray-Ray's favorite topic. However, there was so much to take in. Sometimes, he would not sleep because the thoughts and new information kept his mind spinning. What was it like, he wondered on one sleepless night, to be black in the North prior to the Civil War, when America was allowing thousands of European immigrants to swarm in to jobs and quick citizenship? Blacks still survived. Why were there swarms? What were the Europeans escaping? Other Europeans, right? Even today, he thought, the best strategies for achieving African American economic and social justice are still being debated.

"All we need is a well-designed program, loaded with decoys, that'll allow us to succeed despite changes in leadership," concluded Ray-Ray.

"The leadership must be pure and undefiled," added Tank. "There's too much at stake."

"That's right," Ray-Ray agreed. "No more sleeping with the enemy."

Chapter 17 – Pookie's Tale

It was Friday, July 3, and Pookie already could smell the hellish barbecue aroma from the nine houses across the hot circle of the field. Ebonia's main road was busy with people who were either driving out of town or to the supermarket or to the Saxonville mall. But he had nowhere to go, nothing to do. Tomorrow was just another day. He certainly felt no patriotism, and he would probably try to strangle anyone who would offer to stick even a tiny American flag on his apartment door.

To Pookie, patriots were mere opportunistic goblins within and ushering the first circle of hell. Their insides had been eaten out by the beasts of pride, sloth and inheritance. In the warmth left by their hollowed-out entrails were situated leviathans swimming in bile and purpose. Their stock and store is to elevate an ideal that only they can see. Achieving the euphemism requires entry into a minimum of six additional circles.

From where he stood on his terrace, he could look over the backyards of the houses on the other side of the field and see fathers turning over huge slabs of beef short or pork ribs, the smoke pouring into the sky like fumes from a magic lantern or an ancient sacrifice. But he also failed to see—in those backyards, in those fathers' proud faces, and in the clouds of smoke, which slid along the walls, rubbing its back upon the window panes—a tradition most men longed to share with their families.

All Pookie saw was overspending. He saw that this Fourth of July tradition was only necessary because of the money it put in the pockets of a few. What were these people celebrating? It definitely wasn't the independence of the country. They couldn't care less about the country. A day off work perhaps? He concluded that, yeah, they were the opportunists of Dante's first circle.

Then again: people have always celebrated things that were not kind to their histories, Pookie reasoned. Imagine one summoning up the courage to try to blow up a king and instead ending up as an eternal effigy atop a fire yourself! See yourself as a Wampanoag in what has become present-day Massachusetts, simply enjoying a harvest feast with English pilgrims in the early 17th century. Your circle of hell would include being forced into an allegory of the cave, where you attend the foreshadowing of endless pain and suffering of your people.

As Pookie continued to look out over his terrace, he tried to steady himself. Far be it from him to rain on someone else's charade. If this world was his, he'd place other favorites on the grill. Tasty items like Columbus Day, battle reenactments, and the host of Confederate memorials and celebrations. But he would control anything of consequence.

Then, it occurred to him through the smoke from the community sacrifices that those old, ideal American values could not exist were they dependent upon the majority of the people. The majority was not very patriotic, so it was necessary that an elite develop a means to keep the majority ignorant of their ignorance.

On a patio chair near his terrace door was a collection of poems by T.S. Eliot, half of which he had memorized. He knew "Prufrock" word for word, and he was reciting it as he looked into the backyards, into the etherized, far sky, which reminded him of a long, tedious day, of waiting for someone to love, and to share himself with in the heat of the summer days.

He very much wanted a special young lady, bronze and queen-like, who could, somehow, accept him as he was. He was tired of traveling across town, tired of sleeping with tramps that slept with mental cases, and tired of always having to settle for less when he knew he deserved more. He even had begun to fear that he would not know how to respond to a kind, clean, well-meaning woman who was, say, not from Ebonia and who knew, perhaps, how to treat a man.

Now that the wind was blowing, it seemed that the smell of the barbecue had slipped from his terrace, leaped suddenly to the ground and rested there. *So this is the world?* he asked himself. Where did these fathers find time to sit there, barbecuing their lives and their money away? There had once been a time when he had watched his own father sit in their backyard, turning over large slabs to keep in step with tradition. Then, whenever the end of the month finally came around, his father would have to borrow money from his brother to make ends meet. All because of tradition.

Pookie viewed the Fourth's heavy symbolism to Dante's fourth circle of hell. Oh, the waste made in the pretense of Americanism. Let's put away the patriotism until another time, perhaps Veterans Day. Catch a sale on those ribs and freeze them until Labor Day. Rinse. Repeat.

Every Fourth the same thing happened, until seven years ago his father died in an accident on his way home from the supermarket. People said that he took a chance with a speeding truck coming down Culver Road, his old car cut off in the intersection, and so did his life.

Pookie remembered how blood was all over the package of ribs, how his mother and two little sisters cried and cried, and how all the people were gathered around looking at them, feeling sorry for them.

But Pookie could not cry.

He could only think of what would happen to them now that his father was dead. He was only fifteen then, and his father was just thirty-two. His mother would have to work to support them, and he knew that she would never let him forget it, just as she had never let him forget that she didn't know who his real father was. She would always pull him to the side whenever he was arguing with the stepfather he had as long as he could remember called Dad. She would always tell him not to argue with his stepfather because he did not have to do the things for him that he did.

It seemed that every time he heard those words he despised his mother and even more so his younger sisters, because, it seemed, they had a secret link with his stepfather because of his link to them biologically. It seemed that everyone had some type of attachment to another, but that his mother was determined to see to it that his only real attachment in the family was through her. She always made him careful of what he said to his sisters because she feared that her husband would want to know why this outsider was arguing and fighting his two daughters. Plus, often the two half-sisters used this baffling situation against him.

And what did his mother mean when she said she didn't know who his father was? She couldn't possibly have been such a whore at age sixteen that she didn't remember who threw her legs in the buck just nine months before. She must have been a hot piece of ass in those days. He wondered how many men in town looked at him and said to each other, "That could've been my boy, there." He also wondered how many men must have looked at him and sworn to each other that his mother had the best stuff on the west side of town. But, despite what he felt about her, he knew that he could never erase the fact that she was his mother. He could not bring himself, no matter how hard he tried, to actually hate her.

When he was sixteen, he began working at a drugstore on Ninth Street every day after school. When word got out that the pharmacist was always drunk and was mixing up people's prescriptions, the pharmacist was forced to close up right before the summer. Pookie then cut lawns until the end of October, when the cold started to settle in the South. Then he landed a job at a McDonald's hamburger stand and worked until the Christmas season.

His relationship with his mother improved, but he thought less and less of women as a whole. He would hang around girls who were known for their promiscuity, because he knew that he would never fall in love with them. He figured that if he was incapable of falling in love with women, he could never feel the hurt they could cause a man.

But now he was a grown man, and he still felt the same way about women. One day at Bo Willie's club, even James was unable to change his attitude about his mother and about women in general. James told Pookie about black fathers and their hopeless circles. Pookie, in turn, instructed James about the supply of and the demand for ideals in this wretched society. It was a land that hypnotized black people into believing they were citizens by default because they were doing what so-called patriotic citizens do. *Smoke.*

Chapter 18 – Tony's Tale

"There's no need to be hostile. I did not bring up Carole's name just to put you on the spot or to make you eat your words," Rowan lied.

"I hope not," said Tony Farrington, his nostrils flaring a bit, as if to take in the stench of the conversation and the aroma of the plate of food he was allowed to bring in from next door—but only in exchange for ordering a White Russian. "I think I've learned my lesson. So, there is no need to continue to torture me by bringing up her name. Shit. I think about her enough already!" Tony stared down at the white Styrofoam of sustenance providing his black body with its energy.

Looking back at him was the infused image of a woman he had loved so fiercely that even her breaths seemed tailored to his heartbeat. Because they were made for each other, Tony could not escape the void that consumed him. Their love was supposed to be timeless, designed only with the two of them in mind, always fresh and exciting, daring and sensuous, infinitely expansive yet contained within 270 acres.

"I see her face when no one is around, and I feel like dying when she shows up when I am around people," continued Tony, adding a sense of style even to this tailored white shirt. And, it was like that nearly everywhere he went. One would have thought that he would have had some issues acclimating to Dartmouth. Truth was, though, he made Dartmouth look good, perhaps added some *snap* to its forgotten diversity brochures.

"Remember college commencement out on the field off Wentworth?" he asked Rowan, not waiting for a response. "I looked toward Baker Hall, and I thought I saw her face in the transom window. Then, it seemed that every white woman in the crowd had Carole's face." Rowan rolled his eyes.

"I thought I would lose it right there because, man, I was so scared and didn't know what to do," Tony went on, a slight quiver becoming detectable in his voice. "I kept wondering what would happen to me if all of those faces began to shout about what I had done. I felt like praying that you were sitting next to me to at least tell me that it was all in my head. You were the only person I knew who could talk away all those judgmental white faces, and the many sad faces of my son. But you were sitting in another section, and I had to deal with those faces the only way I knew how. I had to wonder whether or not I had been wrong, and I'm still wondering."

"Right or wrong," commented Rowan, matter-of-factly,

touched by Tony's words but concealing it all the same. "We made a decision when we were at Dartmouth, we acted on that decision, and we can live every single day of our lives fretting about it."

"I know," replied Tony. "But after all these years, every night, before I manage to go to sleep, I see that thin face of hers. Seems like she wants me to know that she is still alive and that she still loves me. That's the agony of it all. How could she love me after that? That's what's driving me up the wall. That is how she is getting even with me. With those sad eyes and that loving smile ... "

"Will you knock it off, man!" insisted Rowan in a shout-whisper. "She is not trying to get even with you. She's worm food."

"Every time I see her, I think of little Tony," stated big Tony, "see him somewhere crying, needing me, and I always feel that nothing can go right for me unless I bring him to me and treat him like he was a part of me—and, you know, he really is. He really is my son, no matter how hard it is for me to accept it. Who would have ever thought this would've happened to me—to us—with all of my 'black this' and 'black that'?"

Tony paused to drink his beer. In his mind, he was a flying African, soaring over a New Hampshire valley, circling around a bell tower like an addicted buzzard. He then slowly looked upward from the table to Rowan, who watched him, hoping his troubled friend would not come to pieces here.

"Rowan," he continued. "You're my friend. What am

I supposed to do? Should I locate my son? I can't forget him—I've really tried to leave him behind, but now I know that's impossible. I don't think I ever will leave him, because I know I love him. What should I do?"

"Tell your wife what happened, and your parents, but don't freak and let loose about what happened to Carole. Say she was in an accident or something. Tell them that despite the fact that his mother was white, you love him and want him. It might be hard as hell to find him after placing him up for adoption in New England so long ago, but you've got connections."

"Yeah," said Tony, now listless, staring into his drink.

"Don't mention what we did to Carole," repeated Rowan emphatically. "That'll just bring everybody down."

"I hope he still has an innocence about him," said Tony, his eyes watery. "He could be cold and cynical, you know."

"Let's just hope his new family aren't terribly insecure," reflected Rowan. "Even better, let's hope that he has been wondering about you, too. Your mother would probably be very fond of him, and even your wife would come around to accepting him because he is a part of you. Go ahead—eat your steak, drink your beer. Things will come out for the better. I'll be right there with you this time."

Tony managed a smile. "Thanks, Freud."

Chapter 19 – Tommy Lee's Tale

"I remember my first love." Tommy Lee smiled. Sometimes, the thought of those young, innocent days brought pleasant memories. "I was really crazy about the chick ... bought her all sorts of things."

"Young love and the quest for the first piece," laughed Enoch. The two were driving over to Saxonville, lured like Odysseus by Circe, to catch the latest Denzel Washington movie at the Samson Theatre.

"It was the next to the last day of the eleventh grade. Remember?" continued Tommy Lee, now taking a right onto the northbound interstate, leaving Ebonia in the distance. In less than a half-hour, they would take the Saxonville exit. "I think the wind was blowing sort of funny that day. Anyway, we were in West End Park, and she told me she had something very important to tell me. She said it couldn't wait any longer."

But Tommy Lee knew they were not in West End Park, as he had told Enoch back then, but rather in her Macbethan living room down in Ebonia Hills.

"Naturally—maybe it wasn't natural at all—I thought that she was going to finally tell me how much she loved me or appreciated the gifts, the little things I'd done for her. Honestly, I actually thought I was gonna get lucky."

"Dee Pashell," recalled Enoch. "Man! Every guy wanted to hit that—me included."

"I know," agreed Tommy Lee, with a hard-won smile. "I guess the odds were against me."

"So what did she want to tell you again? It's been a while," Enoch reminded him. "How exactly did she put it?"

"Well, that day she told me that she *didn't* love me, never had," replied Tommy Lee, trying to keep an upbeat disposition. "In fact, she outright said that she was incapable of loving me. *Incapable.* She didn't want to hurt my feelings, because I had been so nice to her and all. We could be friends, but she could never bring herself to love me.

"And, there was something in the way she said it that made me feel lonely and foolish all at once," said Tommy Lee. He looked over to his left at a farm where a pasture was full of cattle. "But I could not help feeling, you know, that there was something telling me this all along."

"I remember that you were pissed," said Enoch. "Man, I think I would have been pissed ... squared."

"No," Tommy Lee answered, his hands stuck at 10 and 2 on the steering wheel. "Looking back, I was more hurt than anything. I looked into her eyes and ... she still had these angel eyes. Up until that point, I was convinced that we were made for each other. I felt something snap inside of me, and my stomach felt as if it were being ripped open. She said that she was sorry, but life was filled with disappointment, and we all had better face them."

"She said *that*?" asked Enoch. "Why don't I remember you telling me that?"

"Yeah. She said it."

"I mean, like *that*?"

"Yeah. Shit."

"Tough tuna, huh?"

"Oh, yeah," replied Tommy Lee. "I looked into those light brown eyes, never believing they could carry such indifference. I saw the gold necklace around her neck that I had cut lawns for, and she was wearing the watch I had gone to work after school at McDonald's and the Ebonia College cafeteria just to get enough money to buy it for her."

"She always thought you were out of her class, bro," Enoch quickly summed up the situation, "that you were beneath her. She knew she had no feelings all along; it was just a game for her."

"All I felt was just hurt and the added shock that it would take place so coldly," recalled Tommy Lee.

"It's cold in the clouds, my man," said Enoch, matter-of-factly. "You were so far in the clouds that you thought gold could seal the deal."

"Then she said that working in the cafeteria made me smell. The stink from old, decayed food from the wet kitchen floors were in my shoes, and she would rather that smell. The stink from old, decayed food from the wet kitchen floors were in my shoes, and she would rather that I didn't come over to her house after work. She didn't want that smell to get into her mom's carpet."

"Like I said to you back then, it was her loss, man," comforted Enoch, always the gentleman.

"I remember a tear trying to push its way out, and I fought it with everything I had," he said, his hands gripping the steering wheel. "My hurt gradually turned to anger, not at Dee alone but at every woman who even remotely reminded me of Dee."

Enoch's mind seemed to take some celestial stroll. He sat quietly for a moment.

"Well, I did learn to keep my feelings and money to myself," Tommy Lee went on. "I learned from that bad investment. Now that I own a few of my own businesses, there are beautiful black bitches out there, a dime a dozen, just dying to get their hands on a brother who has his shit together!"

"But there aren't too many who want to *help* you get your shit together, though," added Enoch.

"Damn straight!" exclaimed Tommy Lee. "They don't want to work to help put your black ass through law school or medical school! Hell no! They just wanna reap the benefits."

"Does that make us misogynists?" teased Enoch.

"No," Tommy Lee answered, "just careful." They fell silent.

Within the present silence, Tommy Lee buried the fact that he *had* shed a tear, even for just a little while, that night. He had blamed himself and had wrestled most of the night with an angel that had struck him in his pride. He should have gone home from his job, cleaned himself up, brushed his teeth, picked out nice clothes, put on a little cologne, plus a few extras before heading over to Dee's. What in the fuck was wrong with him? You didn't just come as you are to something as fine as Dee, as if you were attending some seedy tent revival!

That night, he had played the fateful event back in his head, and had noted every misstep that had dislodged his destined intimacy. He felt so much like a damn fool. Who was he kidding? Why did he even think he had a chance with a girl like Dee?

Enoch also befriended the silence. He remembered telling Tommy Lee that he deserved better. He had reminded his forlorn buddy that his failures were not the result of anything he had done. Dee would have been a bitch, no matter what. He even had reminded Tommy Lee about jet-black Mr. Gautier, who had worked his charms on his high-yellow wife, who would gladly drink his bath water. Then there was Mr. Glenn, the plumber who probably had his college professor wife climbing the walls at night. He had told Tommy Lee these things because there are a lot of paths to take toward winning women. And, of course, as an insightful high school student himself, he was thoroughly credentialed to provide good counsel.

Within minutes the boyhood friends were taking the Saxonville exit, finding solace in the fact that although they could not win the game, they at least knew when a game was being played.

Chapter 20 – Tank's Tale

She leaned and rested her head on his shoulder and put her hands in his lap. "Why are you treating me so coldly?" she asked.

"I don't make it a practice to open up until I know a person better," said Tank, always to the point. "Especially women. Men's biggest mistakes come from underestimating women." He searched her large blue eyes.

"Would you rather that I open up to you?"

"Yes."

She looked around his living room, eyed a bookshelf full of materials on black nationalism, all the while dangling her feet from the sofa. She made her toes touch the shag carpet as if to aid a damsel who had lost her way in the rug.

When the damsel rested on her feet, she would lift her up, up, up. Then her feet would dangle aimlessly again until another maiden in distress needed her aid.

"Well," she started, "I don't quite know just where to begin."

"I'd say you are a lonely woman," Tank suggested. He believed in aiming for his target. Doing so had spared him much bullshit.

"Yes," admitted Kimberly. "I am indeed lonely. I need someone to talk to, to listen, I guess. You sorta hit the nail on the head then."

"But why are you *here*? Could it be that you have a liking for black men?" He removed her hands from his lap and walked to the kitchen. "I have beer. Would you like one?"

"Yes," she replied. "I would like that very much."

"Bottle or can—or both?" he managed a smile. Anyone could see that humor did not become him. She returned a smile that really had never left her.

"It doesn't matter. But why do you ask me if I have a liking for black men?"

"Actually because it was the simplest way I could put it," he said from the kitchen. He returned and sat down beside her. "Here's your beer and glass."

"Thanks," she said, and poured the beer carefully in her glass, then rising. "To answer your question, I must give you a mitigated yes. I do like black men. But not because I am some cheap white thrill who fantasizes about what it would be like to have black men screw her."

"I never said *that*," said Tank, watching her return to

the couch next to him. He did possess an *iota* of tact.

"I guess it was in the wind. But just because you didn't say it doesn't mean you didn't think or feel it." She lifted her beer again. Tank shrugged and fell silent.

"It's just that I think I have so much in common with some black men. I think you know: the pain, the success wish."

Actually, Tank did not know, then, what she meant, and he really did think and see her as a horny, 42-year-old woman getting her jollies fantasizing about letting black men mount her.

"No," he said, "I don't think I know what you mean."

"I mean," she sighed lightly, "I want to be free to give my understanding or love without having labels or letters placed on my forehead."

For a second that mirrored an eternity, he thought of his Aunt Sage, a revered Black nationalist, whose living room and den were replete with photos of Ida Wells Barnett, Dorothy Height, Lorraine Hansberry, Gloria Naylor and countless other African-American women. She even had found a photo of Ellen Craft, a light-skinned sister who disguised herself as a male enslaver and her darker husband as a valet to travel North and then abroad to some Promised Land.

"But the price of blue-eyed ladies' freedom, understanding and love has too often caused men like me to lose the hairs which tickle their foreskins," said Tank, immediately regretting what must have been a tinge of preachiness and hyperbole in his tone. "You may have been labeled a whore, but we have been castrated."

"I know that that wasn't so very long ago," Kimberly conceded. "But we didn't make the rules." She moved even closer to him. "Why can't two people feel free to share their lust as well as their love? What does black and white have to do with any of it? We don't have to bring the rules behind closed doors. What's to stop us?"

"How about the fact that you are married, Kim?" he countered.

"A state of mind," she quickly dismissed his statement. "Besides, you have someone, too, you big choir boy. If I were *really* married, I wouldn't be here in your arms," she continued, then seductively: "I wouldn't have my hands in your lap, stroking your passion. And ... If you were so worried about not knowing me well enough or my being married, you'd simply push me away. I wouldn't be able to feel your passion swelling and growing. I really wouldn't know that you want me as much as I want you. I wouldn't know that you think you would be betraying all black women by making love to me, right? I simply wouldn't know these things."

She slowly massaged his manhood. "I would not know that your resistance is breaking second by second, or that you now are frightened by the fact that I know your thoughts so well, too well for a flaky white woman, for any woman. But, you see, I am the psychologist of the moment."

Tank, for the first time during the evening, was rattled. His cockiness shattered and his shallow pride thrown against the wall like an old Millie Jackson record, Tank was frightened by both her words and touch. She unbuttoned his shirt and knew that his passion had outrun his resistance. She then loosened his belt and unzipped him, and freed the ancient warrior.

In mere moments, Kimberly became the damsel in distress, being slowly rescued and tortured in her daze by a too-strong knight. She moaned as though a hurt Don Quixote was deep, deep inside of her, begging for mercy as a heartless brute kept beating at him, beating, beating, a never-tiring, never-ending dam of pain deserved.

Tank felt the common pain she had spoken of earlier. He knew he would never be the same after he pulled himself away from her, fig leaves torn asunder, fleshy bravado now but a pillar of salt. He would never see Ray-Ray in the same light, and he would never carry his unbridled research authority among the gang at The Chinaberry Tree without an element of shame.

He was a traitor who had to be punished. He simply passed forward the pain. Tank was still a slave, not because he was someone else's property, but because he was denied the freedom to act naturally. Why did she have to choose him out of all the black men in Ebonia? Why should excitement be given a color anyway? Why couldn't he simply enjoy the moment without wondering whether she would even acknowledge him if she was on her home turf in Saxonville? The complexity of the matter caused him anguish, and he wanted desperately to return the favor.

There was a tightness around his neck, and for a brief moment he felt the room sway, but not in a smooth, singsong way. He thought he saw and felt a glitch, almost as though his mind was processing two parallel dimensions at once. Only he was overcome by an overwhelming tension, the type one gets in the midst of too many unfriendly eyes. For a split second, Tank was one inside the dangling body of L.D. Nelson, suspended from an Oklahoma bridge one warm, still day in May in 1911. Scores of squealing, helpless angels flew in circles at unbelievable speeds around the 14-year-old the very instant his neck popped.

Tank wanted to speak to the other-worldly beings traveling around and around L.D. at the speed of light, causing the dilapidated fabric yet holding on to the boy's swollen ankles to levitate above the muddy river. He wanted them to stop the fuss. They were too damn late. They had done nothing to save that teen. Just as he was about to utter a word from his prison within the suspended prison of L.D.'s body, Tank forced his heavenward gaze downward deep in his eye sockets and made out the body of a lynched woman about 25 feet from L.D. ... *Mama?*

Totally unaware of any angels flying about anywhere or anyhow, though, were the more than 50 white men, women and children on top of the bridge. They were all dressed up in their civilizing Sunday's best and had aligned themselves into a pre-Judgement Day line to await directions from the town's photographer.

Just hours before, some mad men had raped Laura, the hanged boy's mother, left behind her second son, a nursing baby, then dragged her several miles to the bridge. A soft whimper brought Tank back to reality.

"No, please," Kimberly pleaded. "Don't punish me. I'm only a woman."

Chapter 21 – Melvin's Tale

Melvin Hart had been a regular of The Chinaberry Tree for a few years before succumbing to sickle cell disease at age 28. He had been active in the local association, which covered several counties in addition to the one where Ebonia served as the county seat.

From childhood, his had been a life of nothing but limitations, making sure he did not get too hot or too cold or too fatigued. He had to endure jokes about his boniness and his pointed, ant-like head. He was always among the last chosen for teams and often sat among those hapless students placed in the third or fourth reading circles.

While he only worked at odd jobs due to his frequent illnesses, Melvin took part in several fundraisers for the association, especially around Christmas time. About 333 sickle cell clients and association staffers participated in a year-end holiday festivity that was complete with everything from caroling to Santa.

The last Sunday afternoon event he attended before his death was sponsored by the local organization and attracted persons from at least seven nearby counties. Joining the activities were parents from the remote parts of the rural belt, friends and children from Saxonville, which boasted nearly a dozen attendees, Boaz County, Doughtery County, Ebonia County, and others.

Melvin helped to coordinate the effort with the assistance of the association's executive director, and several church volunteers from Ebonia and Saxonville. Mr. Bennie Lewis, the retired superintendent of schools, served as the activity's master of ceremonies.

During the course of the three-hour program, Mr. Lewis led the audience in a caroling medley comprised of a dozen popular holiday songs, from "Silent Night" to "White Christmas." A special heartfelt moment of gratitude was shown to Ethel Mann and a group of Ebonia sorority women, whose innovative and energetic fundraising efforts garnered the local agency more than $144,000. Ethel attributed their success to the countless cakewalks, school events and other means, which included the lion's share from an area bottler. They also credited the Ebonia Wal-Mart for being sensitive to their fundraising quest, as well as the regulars of The Chinaberry Tree.

Melvin, fearing the spread of his disease, never married and had no children. But there were far too few moments dominated by passion of any type. Love was too risky. Every other day belonged to excruciating pain in all his joints, a tightness unlike the Holy Ghost deep in his chest. He often gasped for breath and experienced dizziness and fatigue, jaundiced-looking eyes and often darkened urine. Perhaps the hardest of all was the reining in of the natural, holding steady the sun in the sky as the River Styx ran its course among one's veins. This was Melvin's un-life. This was an awakened world of pure anguish and deniability. Walking into a bar only to drink soda. Challenged to avoid stress in a world piled with bullshit. Constantly witnessing the transparency of adorned insincerity. Knowing the inevitability of death before life has begun. This was Melvin's tale.

Chapter 22 – Ethel's Tale

When Ethel M. Mann was born, Ebonia was hardly a village. The college existed, but only in its most primitive stage. She worked hard to put herself through Ebonia College. Not being a pretty woman meant working even harder. She wore her hair in a short boyish natural, boxed on the ends, not unlike her childhood days on Spring Street.

Little boys always sought the attention of the other girls and tried to tickle them whenever they saw that no adult was looking. But Ethel didn't enjoy moments like those. Instead, they would always tease, "Well, lookit Ethel Mae. Now dat's a new kinda ugly." Sometimes the boys would bark when she passed them.

Those memories were etched in her brain like stone. Her parents struggled to make ends meet, torn between farming and teaching, whichever seemed to promise the best return any given year. Growing up in a shotgun house on Spring Street, Ethel long remembered how her mother would leave early to tend to the kitchen of a white family and how her father would ride out to his father's farm to plow. He had hoped for a steady job teaching at Ebonia College, but the school was struggling, and the pay was a little unsteady.

"There wasn't any stealing, cutting or shooting," recalled Ethel. "You could leave your front door wide open, and nobody'd take a thing. That's how honest and God-fearing folks were. We shared with our neighbors and our neighbors shared with us."

When she was around nine, her mother heard the white folks talking about how the stock market had crashed. It meant little until a few weeks later they said they had no choice but to let her go. Her mother soon found other work at the college and a few years later her father joined her.

A decade passed and Ebonia's little campus, like so many others throughout the United States, was practically void of men during much of World War II. The six men who were on campus during that time had their choice of any woman they wanted, and one was never enough.

Ethel taught in schools in and around Ebonia after graduation. By the mid-1950s, she had completed her master's degree at the University of Wisconsin. By that time, she had established six serious county-wide centers for girls in and around the vicinity of Ebonia. These centers taught young black girls self-discipline, self-respect and independence. They were models upon which several after-school programs would be built in the decades that would follow.

Ethel's centers were touted throughout the community for their thoroughness in addressing the most common problems inhibiting the success of young black girls. She had received the accolades of churches, sororities, fraternities and numerous civic organizations.

She was a rose on the inside, possessing a beauty so powerful as to render listless troubled souls in search of sordid answers. Her empathy consumed any girl she was able to talk with one-on-one. Once won over, they worked feverishly to help her reach as many others as possible.

But like all roses, Ethel also had her share of thorns. For the most part, Ebonia had chosen to ignore them. They looked periodically at her lengthy track record like a credit report; they perused the long list of young ladies who had been helped in the aggregate; and they decided that the ends justified the means. In the war to save lives, sometimes friendly fire occurs.

It was in the cold, cold winters of Wisconsin that Ethel had found that indeed she could be loved by another human being. In that lily-white environment, someone had found beauty in her chocolate skin, had kissed and licked it like the vivid flowers of a honeysuckle vine. The revelation that she could be loved overwhelmed any concern about just who was doing the loving. It was during this journey so far away from home, so foreign to the very world her ancestors owned, that Ethel willingly succumbed to lesbianism.

Years later, even certain members of her sorority would fondly refer to her as "Sister Mann." She continued to brag about how she had helped more young girls blossom into womanhood than any other person, organization or church in Ebonia, the college included. Although many knew of her tendencies, mothers always seemed to push their daughters toward her example. They inwardly prayed that their daughter would not be the exception or spur some sordid desire in Ethel.

Ethel was definitely aware of the rumors. Nonetheless, she prided herself on being Ebonia's oldest lesbian, a distinction and story she wouldn't hesitate to share in an issue of any national magazine. Her live-in lover had died several years ago, leaving everything to Ethel. Of course, some people talked about it, but there was nothing they could do, because, as Ethel put it, "that was Carolyne's wish."

The older she got, the more Ebonia struggled in her grasp. There are many, many things that a woman of means does not have to put up with. Similarly, when it comes to dealing with women of means, there are many things that a small town has to simply grunt and bear. That was the situation with Ebonia, and that was the situation with certain girls that Ethel really liked.

But in its own way, even a very small town has a way of evening the score. Whenever a newcomer would visit The Chinaberry Tree, someone would apprise them of the old butch on top of Virginia's Hill. The men would modernize their jokes as the years passed. Today's version had it that one day old Ethel was sitting in the bar with the other guys, waiting on her drink. When the voluptuous rear end of Ruth Hightower first walked into the bar, three guys—and Ethel—jumped up to offer her their seats.

Chapter 23 – Sonny's Tale

Sonny wept.

Reverend Wright kept hammering away about how Judgment Day would separate it all. The truth would come to light. *Whose side do you want to be on?* It should have been a compelling argument.

The old ladies sang in a low, haunting chant, starting out with ...

Nothing but the blood
Nothing but the blood

Six men clad in white made a semi-circle on a slightly raised platform. They rocked back and forth, heel-to-toe. One, with bloodshot eyes and the voice of Paul Robeson, bellowed out the words in unison, but with no doubt this was his show. His white garment, washed clean, he said, with red blood, smacked of conceit. His holiness was both addictive and troublesome. Sonny looked at the dove at the center of the stage and saw a man riddled by contradiction.

While his eyes were reverent, yet fiendishly seductive, the Reverend's forehead was square and solemn but laced with the brows and lines of a common street hood. But most perplexing of all were his lips. They spoke thunder, as though God were talking right through him. They snarled and curled upward at the ends when speaking of the evils of men. They shouted out over the multitude of St. Luke's, heralding the joys of being in the fold.

Even now, these lips enticed Sonny to rise from the depths of the mourning bench, from the bowels of his blues. Old women tossed their tired eyes in his direction. Next, their lips were hurled downward to the floor just a few feet beside him, right near the bench where he sat all alone one Friday evening. *Da blood! Da blood! Da blood done signed my name!* Fleshy pink lips. Red lips. Even black lips. Opening wantonly and all in time: *Yes! Da blood, da blood, da blood done signed my name.*

Lord! Those loose, loose open lips! Dem tight, tight closed lips—now inching along the side of the pew—open then pursed—slithering toward his right side, where he, too, had been bludgeoned by an angel simply from his ask for meaning. He dared not look rightward, but all the same he knew—he could feel it!—those old lips were methodically making their way up the side of the pew and onto the velvet cushion. *Da blood, da blood, da blood done signed my name.*

Then came the unbearable cadence of a hundred old and very old, dark and very dark women. Their chants had found a dancing partner in the slow, forceful beat of their feet on the church's wood floor, hovering just a few feet over the baptismal pool. *Da blood*, pat-pat, *da blood*, pat-pat, *da blood done signed my name*, pat-pat. *Ohh! Da blood - done signed - my name!*

Sister Carolyne had moaned. She and the Amen Corner had been urging Sonny all week to rise from the bench to be saved during the revival. They wanted him to rise, to walk, to wiggle—anything at all to show some evidence of the Spirit.

The fleshy lips had made their way over the edge of the pew arm and were moving toward Sonny on the mourning bench. He dared not look to his right. His side was really hurting now. Why had something so angelic hurt him so? The approaching, caterpillar-like lips still somehow made the seat vibrate.

He kept looking ahead at the evilness before him. That's how you have to deal with evil ... look it squarely in the face! He envisioned each one of the women who had contributed and placed on loan their lips for this Canterbury journey toward his spiritual torture. Their voices stereophonic now, he felt their sonic words through the seat cushion and in his mind's eye he pictured literally dozens of mouthless, skeletal black women on a canvas marveled by Edvard Munch. They were summoning from some depths and saying in unison:

Rise! Rise!

A pair of lips had found their way within six inches of Sonny's right hip. *How you know it? How you know it? Oh, da blood done signed my name. Oh, da blood done signed my name.*

In spite of it all, it was Reverend Wright's lips that really caused the storm within Sonny. He knew that as long as the storm was raging within him, he would catch hell making peace be still. Like a thousand grandmothers, he knew to sit quietly in place during the storm. For him, he simply had to wait on further instructions from the Lord. So, whether the many pairs of lips came with the morning, with a reliable witness, or bearing a cool and cockroach-infested pool to take away all doubt, he could not rise.

The young boy's peace could not be still. Sonny did not and could not rise. It had nothing to do with the fact that his world at the time wasn't exactly sunny. Rather, it likely had much more to do with that one Friday he came home early from school and saw the same lips now bantering from the pulpit gently caressing his mother's bare breasts on the only Judgment Day he cared to know.

Chapter 24 – Joseph's Tale

Joseph looked at the wall straight across from him. The dusty, large and green rubber plant on his right had a license to poke him in the top of his head, and it did so freely. One huge, stiff leaf had parted his thick, black curls like a switchblade on red, pouting flesh.

Officially, spring was just days away. Slowly, men wearing short-sleeved shirts and light-colored slacks began to fill The Chinaberry Tree on yet another Friday afternoon. Within a half-hour, Mr. Porter and Mr. Butler had all they could handle as a dozen excited men filled and draped the bar's counter, lusting for drinks and any jigger of tantalizing conversation. One by one, Joseph gazed at the drawings of the more than two dozen famous black men on the two-by-three-foot poster on the wall of vanity behind the mountains of liquor bottles. Their hairstyles were impeccable and, although they each sported their own choice of liquor, the poster almost seemed out of place. Perhaps it should have been in a barber shop.

Nonetheless, he could not help noticing it. Each man was unique in terms of shades of skin, head shapes and degree of facial hair. Nearly every hairstyle was different, too. Some hairstyles were square; others slightly round. There were shags, bush cuts with arrows and weird designs on oddly-shaped heads. There were also stately, conservative styles, and others with brown and red tints. But one style reminded Joseph of earlier times, those days in the late seventies when he hot pressed the old afro and wore his long hair down to his shoulders like a Super Fly wannabe. According to the poster, all these styles were possible, or so it would seem, if a brother would only trust his black kinks and green bucks to the orange solution in the brown bottle at the right corner of the poster. But this concoction wasn't about the traditional petroleum-based product often piled on scalps, hair and skin. This was the formula placed in bottles. It flirted with wisdom, masked pain and made life easier to digest.

He caught the only woman among the twelve men staring at him. She sat on the empty stool next to Mr. Porter's end of the bar, on the far, far right. Joseph responded with a slight smile. Satisfied that she had finally won his attention, even if only briefly, Ruth turned her eyes away toward the other men in the room, pretending to ignore him altogether.

The blues briefly interrupted his thoughts about the pseudo-snub. That is, the other regulars in The Chinaberry Tree had settled on a philosophical discussion of the blues as an art form. Leading the discussion was Bo Willie, his voice deep and hoarse, and his cowlicks as invasive as a Baptist collection plate.

"Only a certain kinda person can sang da blues," led off Bo Willie, matter-of-factly, suddenly an Albert Murray on the subject. "It ain't nothin' you can study or copy."

"You got that right," Piper said with a bright grin, his dentures slipping again.

Piper was a reddish brother with freckles and ridiculous-looking, almost orange-colored hair. He was always over-compensating for the misfortune of not having been born black enough. No one's downs were as low as his, nor rhythms as systematic. And, now that the chatter had meandered about the smoke-filled room, had rested on and been kicked from the lips of the Sanhedrin council, he wanted to make it known that he had a monopoly on blues ... and reds, and purples.

For several minutes, as Joseph quietly looked on, Piper hustled away the conversation like the spoiled child who owns the basketball on the project court. He lectured on Little Howling Wolf, B. B. King, Denise LaSalle, Bobby Blue Bland, Johnny Guitar Watson and then a series of lesser knowns. About two and a half drinks later, Bo Willie had managed to wrestle the subject away from him.

"All I'm tryin' to say is dat a man can't sang about what he don't know about," shouted Bo Willie. "All dem folks you talkin' 'bout sang blues true enuff, but most of it come from da soul. Dat's what makes our music diff'rent. We ain't lost our souls yet."

Mr. Lewis, the retired principal and former superintendent, took exception with Bo Willie on the soul issue. He was only a few years younger than Piper, but everyone always addressed him with 'Mister.'

"I wouldn't say that, Bo Willie," said Mr. Lewis. "All people have soul. It might be different from ours, but its soul all the same."

"How so?" asked Bo Willie.

"I mean, I'm sure poor white folks got blues, too," explained Mr. Lewis. "Maybe they should call it 'the pinks.' But, think about it. A poor old trailer-dwelling, pickup truck-driving lowlife who wonders if his hunchback, scraggly woman is cheating on him has the blues, as well. Somehow, it will come out in his music. Likewise with the Irish, or anyone, anywhere, who has had a foot on his neck."

"Well, dat may be," started Bo Willie, determined not to be outdone, "but I still say blues is a black thang. Ain't nobody suffered like we have, so ain't nobody else doin' it justice."

Mr. Lewis decided to let the defense rest, but Brad, who never met a topic he didn't like, took the baton and ran on a track all his own.

"Bo Willie's right 'bout that—we have caught pure dee hell." Most of the men laughed and agreed with the statement. Joseph, however, was exploring other galaxies. Mr. Porter looked over at Piper with a check-that-cat-out look, picking up his inattention like radar. Piper was about to make a smart comment to Joseph, but he was interrupted by Reverend Wright's ramblings.

"Y'all know I grew up in Hardaway," he said. "It was a helluva place to be from. The people were so stupid there. It used to be called *Hardway* when we worked the land as sharecroppers. One day, my old man and some of the other colored farmers accused the Man of cheating them out of money."

"Dat ain't nothing new," added Bo Willie. "What happened den?"

"The white man told them that they were right and that he was awfully sorry. He told them that although he couldn't give them any money, he would give them the letter 'a'. Hardaway."

"You're somethin' else," said Mr. Porter as the men hollered with laughter. "Next," called Mr. Porter to Piper. He snapped his black and white striped bar towel and wiped Piper's glass. He sat the glass down gently, respectfully and filled it halfway with Hennessey.

"A bit more," said Piper. Mr. Porter reached for the bottle and poured the liquid gold on command.

"They thought they were *negotiating*, though," screamed Reverend Wright over the slowly subsiding laughs. "How can a child grow up to be normal coming outta a stupid situation like dat?" The words echoed in Bo Willie's mind. Some men had laughed so hard they were just now wiping away tears. Then, before they could even compose themselves, Bo Willie began to shake and stutter as if speaking in tongues. His cousin, Bubba, rushed to put his arm around him.

"How can ya be normal comin' outta fucked up situation like dat?" Bo Willie repeated, really trembling now. "Black man fightin' here, fightin' ova dare 'gainst dem damn Viet Cong, like we in anotha fuckin' Civil War wid the North 'gainst the South. Dey never gave a fuck 'bout us here, but 'speck us ta fight all dey damn wars. Dey loaded our black asses into combat to git rid of Charlie *and* unda-mined us at da same damn time. Dare weren't nothin' too dangerous dey couldn't stick a black man on it!"

"Don't worry about it, man: you's home now." Bubba started to rock him slowly. "Ain't no more enemies. Ain't no devil beatin' on you. You's home. You's home."

"Our black asses, like good Christian soldiers—happy reconny-zanz missions—somehow, we always on da frontline ... good faithful riflemen fightin' for our country that would have kept us as slaves at home. Overseas, though, we gettin' ambushed, dodgin' booby traps, gettin' picked off by snipers, gettin' wounded and usin' yo' buddy's dead body as a shield!"

The Chinaberry Tree ground to a halt, except for the tinkle of glasses behind the bar. Just like America, business must go on. The mood, in a flash, was somber. Upon entering, every patron would have been willing to engage in any discussion about how well American descendants of slavery were doing in the U.S. The discourse could have easily been taken, with a one drink minimum, to a euphoric state. They could have talked about Blacks in government, on professional teams, running shit in the corporate world, sitting on the Federal Reserve Board, and handling other similar shit.

No. Bo Willie's mental tirade had changed all that. The Chinaberry Tree had run the gamut—and at lightning speed—from Black exceptionalism to a state of racial purgatory.

"You's a hero," encouraged the comforting Bubba, like a giant Black Buddha, his arms still around his friend, still rocking slowly, back and forth.

"I'm not!" Bo Willie was crying profusely now. "I'm a ter'ble person. I da kinda nigga dat turned in Christ. Da nigga that told massa 'bout da escape on da plantation. I'm da one who sicced the white folks on Garvey. I deserved ta be da tunnel rat, pawin' my way through da Viet Cong's piss, shit and traps."

"We is what we is," said Bubba. "That can be said 'bout everythin' on this earf." It was difficult to tell whether the fine lines thrown throughout Bubba's face were a result of his seemingly good nature or from too many impromptu counseling sessions like this one. Of course, he didn't mind Bo Willie. But, in fact, he did find himself doing this shit too often. Surely, with all the intellect out there, even in this place, there had to be someone else out there equipped to talk a man off a cliff.

Bubba looked slowly around The Chinaberry Tree. The patron's visages had become the hollowed-out shells that they, perhaps, had always been. A pathetic heap of masked bravado. A dozen or so generations of charcoal-colored runners on a sticky tar track of life, always getting their feet deeply mired in—and ruthlessly pulled back by— time. While simultaneously comforting Bo Willie, Bubba performed his own reconnaissance mission. He looked around and found Butler and Porter behind the bar. If it were left up to him, he'd place them among the war's medical personnel. They'd help the wounded and risk it all, though under fire, for the safety of the patrons. He saw Lewis and Brad as members of the medevac crew in a smoldering combat zone, numbly aware of the dangers of enemy ground fire. In Piper, Bubba saw a court jester likely only fit for a USO show in Long Binh, Da Nang or Saigon. After that, you'd have to fly his trifling ass back to the states.

As for that shyster Reverend Wright, Bubba would place him among the frontline infantry riflemen. He could see the pastor as a young military buck, hardly an enemy gunshot away from shitting his pants. The scared religious man would have been among the thousands upon thousands of black soldiers scooped up in the Army's visionary and mandatory diversity program. A perfect specimen for the annihilation that hundreds of years on American soil could not accomplish. Indeed, Bubba had seen a million men just like him back in 'Nam. He'd learn to see all of them just as the powerful saw them: dispensable. No? Then disposable. *No, again?* Then, definitely apt for pruning.

"It's gonna be alright," Bubba said to Bo Wille. He pictured Reverend Wright again as a cocky, singing 18-year-old in the 2nd Battalion and 7th Cavalry Regiment prior to the Battle of Landing Zone Albany in mid-November of '65. Humph. *No one* sang at Ia Drang. Before he fixed his vision on Ruth and the colorful newcomer, Joseph, Bubba had a change of heart about Reverend Wright and pulled him out of the shit in which he had mentally placed him. The Reverend, too, would have been little more than a child, picked out from a barrel that was about to be tossed out in its entirety anyway. He would have been ideal for killing off. Young. Fit. Poor. Black. Barely educated. Dumb enough to believe they were purely American.

Bubba had trouble placing Ruth and Joseph in the war. His brain kept getting weird vibes about her, similar to the chaos that ensues when an old television dial is stuck between two channels. When he looked at Ruth, his meter and judge of character ran akilter. At one end of the spectrum was a humble Nubian queen and at the other end was a bonafide Alabama-grade cunt.

The nerve-wrecking goings-on were not lost upon Joseph. The red scene had snapped him back into reality. True, fairly new to The Chinaberry Tree, Boy Blue had not learned that Bo Willie was a Vietnam vet who often wrestled with actual and imagined demons, which meant demons all the same.

"The real question is," began Mr. Lewis, valiantly trying to return normality to the gathering of heads on the subject of soul, "who will carry on the tradition? I don't see it with this younger generation."

"Now, you know, that is something to ponder," agreed Mr. Porter.

"The young folks nowadays ain't had it hard enough," a slowly, self-reviving Bo Willie stepped in. "They don't know what to sang 'bout."

"It's gonna be like tap dancing," commented Piper. "We'll have to get white folks to re-teach us a dance that we started."

By now Bubba had begun to move back to his seat. He had done his job, performed it well. In essence, he had thrown the cape over James Brown. Bo Willie was becoming his old self now and was ready to start meddling again. "What 'bout you, young college buck in da rainbow shirt and dem tight polyesta pants!" snarled Bo Willie. "I betcha don't know nothin' 'bout the blues." Mr. Porter had finished pouring a new soul in Piper's glass. Piper looked at himself in the mirror and was gradually becoming proud of what he saw, gray and all. He pulled a small comb out of his shirt pocket and began to part his hair down the middle, causing an angry Red Sea that could barely hold back the kinks of Africa.

Bo Willie looked over at Piper's newly parted hair, and loudly announced to all that Mr. Porter had succeeded in bringing old pussy back to life, and it was sprawled atop Piper's head. As Piper stepped down from the stool with a chuckle, Mr. Porter looked at Joseph, held up a bottle of cognac, and said, "Anyone?" Sometimes, the men gave up their turn at the booze if doing so meant an opportunity to place an unsuspecting visitor in the hot seat.

"You prob'ly ain't went through jack, huh, liddle punk?" coaxed Bo Willie.

"Don't be getting rough," cautioned Mr. Porter. Piper had paid the bartender, reached for his cane, but then decided to hang on for the crossfire on the Ides of March.

"I wouldn't say that," Joseph answered, trying to be

polite in a setting where such niceties often were rare.

"Oh, I woodn't say dat," mimicked Bo Willie. The other men in the bar laughed. "What have you bin through?"

"Nothing ... "

"Doggone right! *Nothing!*" shouted Brad, this time uncharacteristically.

"I'm just here for my daddy's funeral." The room fell silent. It was a throwing the gavel type of silence. A drop the mike type of silence. If the Man Upstairs had to save the city on the goodness of the souls in The Chinaberry Tree at that moment, then several black asses would have been toast.

"You're right," humbly commented Joseph. "I haven't been through any trials. I should have, though, and I realize that now."

"We're sorry ... " began Mr. Butler, from his noble post behind the bar. "We didn't know ... "

"That's okay," said Joseph. "I ran away from home to live with an aunt in Philadelphia when I was fourteen. It was just my dad and me back then. You all probably can remember back to the day of the blind man and his streetwise wife here in Ebonia, right? My Mama left when I was eight. She couldn't take it."

"Was he beating the two of you?" asked Bo Willie, straddled over a folding chair.

"No, a physical beating would have been welcome—nothing like that," Joseph went on. He looked around in disbelief. This was a small town. Everyone knew every other person's business. Why didn't they simply cut the bullshit? "He had this disorder that made him blind, and sort of shriveled up the flesh on his face. It was difficult for him to breathe, and sometimes he couldn't talk.

"After Mama left, Daddy fumbled around the kitchen and cooked for the two of us. He would burn his fingers trying to iron my clothes. It was important that he took care of his own, you see. He sold the car Mama left behind and sent me with neighbors to buy the clothes that were in style. He made me sit down with him to listen to religious tapes or to read him the Bible.

"I led him into the pulpit and heard him preach to the church he had gone to from the time he was a boy. I walked him to Piggly Wiggly to buy our groceries. I helped him change his clothes and matched his colors for him."

Mr. Porter silenced the glasses. Piper sat quietly in a corner chair near the hat racks. Bo Willie stared at the floor, while Mr. Lewis seemed to stare into Joseph's mouth. Ruth and the other patrons in the bar sat at attention.

"I really don't know why I ran away." Joseph's voice began to break. "I had been stealing from him all along. But this time I had saved enough to get away. I don't know why ... "

Bo Willie shifted in his seat, then decided to stand up. He strutted over to the poster with the pictures of the two dozen men. His wrinkled tan trousers still held the imprint of the folding chair he had abandoned on the far side of the room.

"I guess I got tired of all the stares, or maybe it was the smells," said Joseph, a tear trickling down his face and onto his multi-colored shirt. "I was too proud, even as a child. It had become too hard to hold my head up. But Daddy always acted like nothing was wrong, like it was perfectly natural for me to lead him to whatever place he wanted to go, as if no one was treating us any differently. His spirit never wavered.

"I was the kid with the ugly, hideous father. Teachers would tell me that I didn't have to bring can goods to give to the less fortunate. Then, I finally began to realize that it was because it was understood that *I* was the less fortunate—*me!*

"I don't know why I ran away," Joseph repeated, his eyes staring into a barren, colorless nothing. "The social workers—a bunch of them. Maybe it was the fucking social workers—just a paycheck from poverty themselves! They would come by the house, to study us, like we were a test they had to pass to validate themselves. Then the church people, all the praying and preaching and pity.

"I couldn't take it," said an unmerry Joseph. "I should have been stronger, but I wanted to live a life like every other kid. What a stupid situation, huh?" He looked over at Bo Willie. "So, I left a man who believed in me even though he had not seen me. He constantly gave, and I constantly took.

"Now I'm back ... too late ... to see the most beautiful, most colorful human being I've known," sobbed Joseph, unable to retrieve himself from his well of emotion. "I just want a little Jack Daniels, and a little Fresca, please," he directed Mr. Porter.

"My blues song would be about running away from the one you love, I guess. Or, maybe it's about refusing to hand over your childhood. I guess you can't put that kind of thing in a blues song ...

I left my old blind daddy
to make it on his own
So, now I'm back in Bammy
Out here all alone

Joseph brutally mocked their blues. He repeated his refrain. Now, his eyes worked their way around the room, aligning themselves with the eyes of a dozen men and a queen. Piper stared back, but soon lowered his eyes, outdone. Bo Willie, when it was his turn to return Joseph's gaze, simply smacked on a piece of gum and tried to minimize the situation in his own little mind. Mr. Lewis was motionless, without a rationale.

Mr. Porter just hummed. Finally, Joseph fixed his gaze on Ruth, who had teased him before.

I's got betta things to do
Than play wid little girls
Who bat their eyes and fashion lies
Behind a head of curls.

I left my old blind daddy ...
I was ashamed, you see.
But, oh my soul, he's on the roll
Of a better place to be.

As he finished, he gave The Chinaberry Tree another once over. Silence. He knew then that vengeance was his. The twelve brothers were silent, almost repentant. In the span of only minutes, they had become prisoners of his

Egypt. He had transformed a hostile Apollo Club into his wanting, swollen chambermaids.

Mr. Porter proceeded to top off the second round of the thick blocks of ice and Jack Daniels. The brimstone rolled down his throat like the final stone for Sisyphus.

"That'll be eight dollars, son," said Mr. Porter nearly twenty minutes later. Joseph reached for his hip pocket and pulled a ten from this tri-fold wallet.

"Keep the change," he said. He noted his hapless chambermaids, thrown gap-legged around the room. He looked briefly at himself in the mirror against the wall. "Daddy would have been proud. Take it easy, gentlemen ... lady." He held his head back as if raising himself above the intolerable and strutted out the door.

"My daddy lost an arm in the war ... " started Bo Willie.

Chapter 25 – The Imposter's Tale

The little bell above the door jingled merrily as I entered The Chinaberry Tree around six o'clock on the cloudy evening of June 6.

"What's up, Arnold?" three to four members of the group said in greeting when they saw me enter. It felt good to walk in at a time when everyone there knew my name.

"What's up, fellows?" I replied, as had been the custom over my three years in Ebonia. Thunder rumbled in the background. I decided to sit in one of the seats by the front door. It allowed me a full view of the room to quietly observe what, at the onset, seemed to be a good piece of dialogue. I saw Tony sitting in a booth looking on but isolating himself.

A group of regulars were having a fired-up discussion about what it means to be black in America. It was familiar territory, but this conversation seemed to be building a momentum of its own that actually could result in someone's enlightenment.

"We'll never get anywhere as a people until we start doing things for ourselves," exclaimed Reverend Wright. "That's what I tell my congregation from the pulpit. They need to know about the Word of Life and—"

"—The game of life," concluded Enoch. "You can't win it. Just have to play it."

"That's loser talk, there," Brad jumped in. "The game can be won, just as Reverend Wright is saying, but you *have to* get there on your own. You can't have your leaders jumping in front of TV cameras all the time for their own glory."

"My point! That's just my point," continued Reverend Wright. "You have to have a strategy, and not everyone on the planet needs to be monitoring your strategy. Part of the approach has to be re-educating black people about their history."

"Amen to that," Brad chimed right in. "The history taught to blacks our age came from a point of view that virtually ignores the existence and contributions of almost an entire continent."

The bell jingled again. Co-owner Bo Willie entered. "Let my people go!"

"What's up, Bo Willie!" several members of the group sang out.

"See," explained Brad, always a self-appointed expert

on whatever subject he could form two sentences around. "While the world loves Egypt, it will also lead you to believe that Egypt has no attachment to Africa, that it's just sitting on the northeastern part of it because there was nowhere else to place it at the time."

"Right," said Reverend Wright. "But, hell, the Nile of the pharaohs flows out of Ethiopia."

"Burundi," murmured Ray-Ray, a sudden ghost in the room.

"And you mean to tell me that no Ethiopian brother," started Piper, building up steam, "sitting along the banks of the Nile in days of yore, ever said to himself, 'Damn, I wonder what that Egyptian pussy feels like. I believe I'll sail up this here river to see if I can get me a piece.'"

Mr. Butler and Mr. Porter laughed and alternatively wiped the bar and shined glasses for a special customer who was still expected. My good friend James entered the bar, said hello to everyone, then sat next to me. Within a few seconds, a young guy from the local college, just barely legal, came in. His baggy pants were practically falling off his butt, and he found a seat within the room without acknowledging or greeting anyone.

"They had a civilization, too," summed up Brad. "And, they set a standard of performance unparalleled by the rest of the world."

For the next thirty-three or so minutes, the conversation took a turn, with Bo Willie adding his two cents, when he could. I held short side conversations with James off and on throughout. Even borderline militant Baggy Pants, obviously a new summer session student, jumped into the conversation as if he owned the damn place. I was certain it would only be a matter of time before The Chinaberry Tree elite acquainted him to protocol.

Consensus on the need for proper history lessons led the established bar advisors along a path that focused on Egypt as a black African civilization; the Egyptian influence on Greece; Egypt's impact on later cultures in Africa and Europe; and their assertions that African civilization had been intentionally covered up. Baggy Pants' only contributions were: "Man, that's deep."

"When I was in Bien Hoa in 'Nam," recalled Bo Willie, "I had just made out with this liddle prostitute. It was some good stuff, I'll tell ya. I was young and arrogant."

"No!" exclaimed Brad. "You?"

"It is easy to think dat you can stake a claim on sump'n just 'cause you hittin' it," Bo Willie continued, not missing a beat. "Her English wuz pretty good, and she kinda had this thing for always lettin' me know dat she was more than just a whore who let black men poke her, y'know."

Again, *whenever* Bo Willie talked, The Chinaberry Tree listened. Baggy Pants seemed to pick this up right away. Reverend Wright, finally pouring himself a drink from one of Mr. Porter's bottles, fixed his eyes on Bo Willie's mouth.

"What'd she say?"

"You know, foreign women do some pretty interesting things," added old Piper, trying to catch up with the conversation. "During my short service in World War II, I had a foreign woman in Texas."

"I said some shit I woodn't have said to any utha woman," Bo Willie went on. "I looked over at her nice, petite liddle body and dem liddle firm, perky titties, and I got hot all over again. So, I climbed back on top of her without caring what she thought. I was working on it like a Mandingo."

"Talk to me," prodded Mr. Butler, not missing a stroke as he poured Seagram's into Enoch's glass.

"It started gettin' good to me, and I was 'bout to cum," said Bo Willie, his eyes glazed over from the memory, a slight, painful smile across his lips. "As I was strokin', I asked her, 'How you like American dick?' She sorta grunted. Then she angled her head so that she could find my eyes with hers, and she asked, 'How *you* like it?'"

"What did she mean?" asked Trent, following an abrupt laugh. "Ooo, they're playing Billie Holiday on the jazz station. Mr. Porter, turn that up a bit."

"I finally asked her, but not 'fore I was finished," Bo Willie replied. "I didn't want to know what she meant so bad dat I wood mess up a good nut, know what I mean?"

"Know exactly what you mean!" shouted Piper, warming up to rare form. Everyone bellowed with laughter.

"She was tellin' me dat America was screwin' me," Bo Willie continued. "She asked me some shit 'bout how come in da early 1900s America let in dees thousands of immigrants from England, France, Ireland and utha places, but nobody at all from Africa. I told her I didn't know. I remember even while she was lying' there talkin' all serious like, I was steadily strokin' my thang so that I could ride that ass one more time.

"She said that it was 'cause it didn't need no mo' black folks. They purpose had been served. She told me dat black soldiers didn't know shit 'bout demselves and even less about what America had done to dem. By decidin' who wood be 'lowed to enter the country and how many, she said, America locked blacks in as a minority, no matter how many nigger babies they'd ever have. Chances to build old money to pass on was gone foreva, 'cause blacks couldn't play da game then. She said as long as we tie our past to America's past, we'd never know how to make America work for us."

There was an unsettling silence of contemplation.

"But dat's not the killa," added Bo Willie. "Even doe she was talkin' some deep shit, I was so young and cocky, all I was thinkin' 'bout was easin' this third hard-on off in her. She said a lotta shit that night. Dat black folks were just like da chinaberry tree in America. Dey beauty and shade wasn't appreciated, she said. Dey kids are allowed to fall on da ground, be stepped on, smashed and den da few dat are picked up are used as ammo and poison for white men's wars. Like the chinaberry tree, blacks in America are in da worst place on earth to flourish and be a tree. She said black children, the chinaberry fruit, were supposed to be treated specially, da poison dat dey innocence pulls out da ground to save da world is supposed t' be squeezed outta dem, den da berries should be nicely colored an' worn around da wrists, necks and ankles of an enlightened nation, da savior an' da saved. What really woke me up was when she sat up in da lotus position, looked down at my thang an' den straight in my eyes an' said, 'I be whore in Vietnam, but not nigger in America.'"

"That's some tough medicine," commented Piper.

"That's deep," added Baggy Pants, as if on cue.

"It simply brings us full circle to what we were saying a while ago," stated Reverend Wright. "A look at African American history and the colonial history of Africa should show us that our advancement is in our own hands."

"Our *next* advancement," suggested Brad. "We were advanced before our ties to America. That's what Miss Saigon was saying. But she was perfectly able to ignore the hundreds of thousands of prostitutes in her own country back then and pretend she was doing your black ass a favor."

"By da way," interjected Bo Willie, "I did break dat third one off in her anyway. For Africa!"

"For Africa!" shouted the citizens of Ebonia.

***

Usually, I was a silent observer during most of these conversations. But I had developed a feel for the sentiments of Ebonia, had interacted with so many of the regulars on many subjects, and had blended into the community so well as to become a full-fledged member.

"I think we are focusing too much on the black and white of the issue as opposed to concentrating more squarely on making our people more economically competitive," I reasoned.

I glanced about the room from my usual seat at the front corner of the bar, a seat I had chosen so that I could keep a pulse on the entirety of the surroundings. I searched the faces for the first likely ally. Good natured Piper wore a smile and a puzzled look. Person by person, with speed to break the sound barrier, I canvassed the place for a voice of agreement. I finally looked at James next to me, as if searching for a meaning behind the silence.

James, a kindred spirit instantly aware of my nervousness, gently touched my wrist and said, "Breathe."

I did. I was even beginning to settle in my seat for friendly fire when Bo Willie, seemingly holding his tendency to erupt at bay, scooted forward on a recently drawn barstool. That meant one of two things. Either he was positioning himself to leave or he was just about to dive feet first into someone's rectum.

"*Our* people?" he asked, the brass W dangling on his chest, accentuated by the black T-shirt. "Why you say, '*our* people'?"

Immediately, all the brown faces in the bar were staring at me, and what they saw without a doubt was an embarrassed, blue-eyed white man with stringy dark brown hair in need of trimming. "Well," I fumbled to explain. "I see your struggle as my own ..."

"Uh-oh," uttered Baggy Pants, the little instigating bastard.

"And what struggle might that be?" asked Reverend Wright. "We know you seem to like collecting struggles to place in your little arsenal for future use, I guess."

"The one for advancement, of course," I countered, "that when it comes down to the American pie, everyone gets a rightful piece."

"Now dat's interestin'," began Bo Willie, stroking his

chinny-chin-chin. "All dis time, I thought dat all you cared about was makin' sure you had free access to a piece of black booty."

Ouch! I felt James squirm next to me, and pitied him. Only a fool—or someone like Brad—would try to go toe-to-toe with Bo Willie, even for a friend. I heard Baggy Pants mutter to Trent something that sounded like, "White boy's in trouble."

I can beat this, I thought. I also had some very concrete ideas in my head, but being thrust into the spotlight by 24 eyes had merely unnerved me.

"I believe that in order to hold the interest of the lives of young African-American men and women today, we—" Damn. Did I just say *we*? They're going to have my ass for lunch ... Too late now—"we have to shed light on the 'whys' that have had a bearing on their parents and grandparents. I believe we can open the door to them by dealing with the immediate past as opposed to the ancient past."

"Go on," coaxed Bo Willie, like the Big Bad Wolf urging the little pig to eat its vegetables. "Dis is gettin' good." I felt like the little Vietnamese hooker must have felt as Bo Willie was greasing himself up for the third time.

"Well," I continued, more afraid that I would soon begin to ramble incoherently. "Just th-think about the overwhelming black achievements in entertainment, sports, politics and the formation of a significant middle class. That's something that has happened primarily within the last few generations. They can sink their teeth into that. While arguments about ancient Egypt and Greece are important, it's unlikely that the young folks will have an opportunity to visit these places or study them in-depth to discover that truth for themselves. However, no one can deny the resilience of the African American community, because it wasn't effectively allowed to enter the race for resources for centuries.

"That meant that had someone's great-grandfather not been restricted," I went on, "his opportunities to pursue wealth could have positively impacted his family's choices. That means that if great-grandpa had made a million, then grandpa and pa might have also been millionaires. So, when someone was wronged a hundred years ago, you can't just say, 'It wasn't me. I wasn't there. I had nothing to do with it, so don't make *me* pay for it.' Few people of any race will deny *their* claim to their ancestors' millions, regardless of how those millions were made. No one says, 'I had nothing to do with it. I didn't earn it. Don't give it to me. I don't deserve to live so well because of someone else's sweat or sins.' But if we can inherit assets, then surely we can inherit liabilities. We pay for our fathers' sins, as well."

I could sense that the stares were beginning to ease a bit. With a few more thoughtful maneuverings, I could stir myself clear of the abyss. It would be touch and go, with no room for any slip-ups. I looked around the room again. Relax, I told myself. *You know everyone here. They won't hurt you.*

"Speakin' of *your* father's sins," started Baggy Pants. "Who was that fine little light brown-skin honey I saw you talking to near the white college?"

The stares that had begun to die down intensified again. Damn that little punk!

"That was probably Ruth," I said, dismissing him. "So, an accurate recording of the immediate past and the present from an African-American perspective could prove an important legacy, too. Throughout history, people have been and still are defined by their land of origin, their history and culture. French history and culture points to France. Irish lore and heritage leads back to Ireland. Italian art and foods stem from Italy."

So far, so good. They were listening intently. Bo Willie looked as though he could have been patted on the head and tucked in for a nap. I was on the right track. Success in this undertaking would ensure that I was a full-fledged Ebonian.

"The term *black*, then," I went on, "says more about how an individual looks than who he really, *really* is. That's something African-American historian John Henrik Clarke, from Alabama by the way, used to preach. We all know how America likes to label people, and after it labels them, it dismisses them."

"Amen to that," said Piper.

"Likewise, all of the other terms manufactured for African Americans, including colored and Negro," I rolled on, "simply provided America's massive immigrant population a common group to claim superiority over."

"Say it, say it," cooed Reverend Wright. With these words of encouragement, I felt the tide turning. All I needed to hear was the voice of Bo Willie, and I'd be on my way to Ebonian citizenship. I simply had to tread lightly.

"Ruth, *who*, my man?" tormented Baggy Pants.

"Did you say, *Ruth*?" Brad asked, as though tasting an unfamiliar dish. "Ruth Hightower?"

"Arnold! You ain't bonin' dat foxy Ruth, are you?" asked Bo Willie, tone and demeanor undetectable. He looked around quickly. "Where she be? Her fine ass ain't here today, is she? Wasn't she here earlier?"

"We just talk," I said, my heart in my throat, my citizenship slipping a notch. If I could just make a quick transition back to the discussion at hand, all could still be saved.

"With your hand between her legs?" asked the smart-ass Baggy Pants. "In that little eating place near the white college in Saxonville, I saw you with your hand between her legs."

Damn him!

"I don't recall that, but we d-do talk from time t-to time." I felt myself stuttering a little, another crack in the Coliseum. "She d-*does* work in Saxonville, you know. And I *have* been working on my doctorate there for only the past three years, you know!" I had to remain cool. I couldn't let that little thug make me lose the relationships I had worked so hard to build. Perhaps now he'd shut his trap!

"Are you Catholic or Protestant?" asked Baggy Pants.

"What?"

"Catholic or Protestant?"

"Protestant," I answered, almost snidely. "Why?"

"Have you been poking your anglo in Saxonville, Protestant?" he retorted. The 24 or so eyes squinted as nervous teeters stretched into outright laughter, which filled the room. Trent slapped his thighs as if having a spasm. Piper's dentures must have slipped, and Bo Willie and Brad looked at me as though they wondered what was taking me so long to walk the plank.

"She was *just* in here—" noted Mr. Porter.

"And she packed all of that nice behind into this seat here," added Mr. Butler.

"So, Mr. Blue Eyes' been slyly bangin' Ruth Hightower," smiled Bo Willie, and I knew the chances of getting back to the subject were lost now. "Kinda like dat brown sugah, don'tcha?"

I looked over at James, who shrugged without moving a muscle. I really didn't know what to say to Bo Willie. What should I say?

"You ain't gotta say nothin'," Bo Willie answered for me. "I *know* it's good. You couldn't help yo'self. You's a man, too. Seein' all that plump booty walkin' 'round in a black wonderland would make any man crazy."

"Have mercy!" exclaimed Mr. Butler.

"It's one thang you didn't factor in, doe," Bo Willie said, looking me directly in the eyes.

"What's that?" I asked, having given up any claim to innocence and a key to the city. Baggy Pants had shattered my confidence, and I thought everyone was holding a hand of aces against me.

"Well, gettin' a piece of black booty doesn't mean you have suddenly got some new understandin' of blackness in America," said Bo Willie, not unlike the scene in the movie Mahogany, when Billie Dee Williams was about to backhand the shit out of Diana Ross. "Think you some schemin' China-man in Africa? It only means dat Mr. Arnold here's got to experience first-hand the tender booty of a partic'lar woman at a partic'lar place and at a partic'lar point in time."

"In other words," jumped in Brad, "the black experience didn't transfer from her hot box through your white pecker and up to your white brain, causing your baby blues to see the pain of the African Diaspora more clearly. Got that, Benedict?"

Benedict? I suddenly and rightly felt under attack for the first time. Rather than being in a position of control from my perspective in the room, I was on the hot seat and didn't like it one damn bit. Baggy Pants had started this shit. That smug tadpole! That uppity n—..."

"The way you use 'our' and 'we,' you've probably had more black stuff than Ruth's," reasoned Bo Willie. *Guilty again,* I thought. "The only thing—"

"*Only* thing!" bellowed Brad, now Bo Willie's unlikely ally.

"The only thing you know fer sho is dat you like black women," Bo Willie summed me up. "Nothin' expert 'bout that. Don't take no Ph.D. to figure dat out. A few pieces of black ass and now you're ready to set policy for us?"

"I don't think he—" James began.

"I don't think I was talkin' to you," cut in Bo Willie, his words a double-edged sword. He turned his attention to me again. "I've had some Vietnamese stuff, an' I ain't tryin' to run Vietnam. And, by da way: *somebody* just happened to ease into dat journal you got, and they say you make *ev'rybody* a sex freak!"

Baggy Pants wore a broad smile, obviously enjoying

himself. He looked at me and then toward all of the others and said in a feigned, broken voice, "Can't we all just get along?"

With the exception of James, it seemed as if everyone in the bar took a turn kicking me, primarily for assuming that being *tolerated* by the community was the same as *belonging* to the community. There had been a few whites who actually *belonged* to Ebonia. They stuck it out, because they were genuine. I probably wouldn't be a part of that group, because I thought I was "slick," Bo Willie said. I wasn't bringing *anything* to the table, yet I was just "sopping up" black experiences and taking the bread, the gravy and the plate with me, commented Brad.

Mortally wounded for the first time, I quietly sat and festered as Mr. Porter served me my glass of scotch. As I swiveled back around on the stool to heal, my eyes tried to lock in on all of my attackers. But their attentions had gone on to other things. Even Bo Willie and Brad were looking like innocent choir boys. It was as if the whole scenario was in jest, with no real harm intended. Piper left with a "Take it easy, Arnold." Trent exited with, "Hit it from behind!" and Enoch said, "Stay in the game, player."

I tried to fix my eyes on Baggy Pants, but he avoided my gaze. When Mr. Porter had finished, I tipped him, and said goodbye to the remaining patrons. "Be good now," Bo Willie called back.

"Later, my friend," answered Brad.

"I'll talk with you later, my brother," promised James.

The bell above the door of The Chinaberry Tree jingled one last time as I stepped into the hot, humid evening air.

When I returned to my apartment, I plopped down on the sofa. I thought about the sound thrashing I had just taken at The Chinaberry Tree. Inside, I knew there was some merit to Bo Willie's verbal lashing. It still carried a sting.

I had been offered a full-time job and the rank of assistant professor of American history at the black college in Ebonia. The pay wouldn't be much to write home about, but it would allow me the chance to be comfortable. Over the years, I had accumulated a massive collection of files with information about African-American achievements since the Civil War. I had perused nearly every document within the humongous collection at nearby Tuskegee on lynchings. I had boxes and boxes of materials covering black sports, politics, inventions, education, business and other subjects.

I had everything I needed to tell the fascinating story of the life of African-Americans, who my research led me to believe were the true Chosen People. For all these years, I had collected and collected, hoping for the deeper motivation that would force me to stop and pull it all together. As Brad had said, I had sopped up the gravy from the black experience until the dish was empty. At least, I thought it was empty. I never learned all there is to know because all there is to know has to be experienced, as well.

In short, I had nearly everything in my capacity to tell a story that needed to be told. This became increasingly clear, particularly as I recall the first conversation I had at Ethel Mann's house. I had heard that she had done some great things throughout her life, but I did not want to concentrate on that. Here was this fascinating woman who had done so many things with absolute perfection and who was an example to all. But what did I want from her? I wanted her to tell me about her lesbianism. I remember the obviously disappointed look on her face, accompanied by a light sigh.

"What's wrong?"

"You seem to have this thing for looking into folks' underwear," she answered point blank. "If you're only looking for stains, then go through their laundry. At least there people have acknowledged the stains and have thrown them aside and moved on to clean them or get something new. A person like you tends to find what he's looking for—even when it ain't rightly there. You make more of a mess in your quest to find what's underneath than would be there if you were simply content to recognize that knowing everything is knowing nothing. I know people like stains and dirt—especially when it's somebody else's. But there ain't no great love for a panty sniffer, either. That sums up lesbianism, and that's all I got to say about it. If sniffing underwear makes me such a bad person, what does it make of you?"

I had no doubt that the women and men at The Chinaberry Tree were my friends. But, sometimes, only friends can tell you what you really need to hear. Ethel had fired a warning shot that I ignored. Baggy Pants was the catalyst that brought everything to a head, and I began to see him differently. He would probably stumble into my class one day, find me sitting at the desk and literally piss on himself. I'd try to calm him.

Chapter 26 – The Reckoning

On July 7, Ruth and I were scheduled to meet at our usual place in Saxonville around 7 p.m.

Two yellowhammers launched from their brief perch atop a yard sign in front of Chaucer's Inn, opening their sunlight plumage and ascending to the branch of a sweetgum tree, where five others awaited them. The park adjacent to the tavern displayed fervent attempts at a medieval façade of 14th century England. Seven stone-like benches were placed around a small courtyard. Sidewalks went north and south and east and west in the center, forming a cross. A quaint bookstore, a coffee shop, a sandwich shop and the Chaucer's Inn served as anchors for the walkways. It was approaching sunset, yet there was still a brightness outside the tavern's window that made the stoic atmosphere on the other side look all the more austere. Inside was a coldness that lingered. It seemed to represent a frigidity of soul, a harnessing of the imagination for a later that never came. The chairs, the benches, and even the old chest in the corner near the bar—all were void of feeling. It was as though the tavern had a curse on it that nothing inside its wall could emit one iota of creativity.

Perhaps the only exception was a large vivid painting behind the bar depicting what were likely the two dozen pilgrims from the Canterbury Tales. I found myself staring at the images on the painting, slowly checking out their intricate designs, one by one. I almost gasped when I reached one image that seemed to stare back at me. It was Crazy Hezekiah! He was looking directly at me!

"Whatcha having, guy?" asked the bartender. Unbalanced, I made every effort to regain my composure.

"I'm waiting on a friend to arrive," I said, "but I guess I'll have a swig of gin over ice."

After I downed the drink, following several attempts, I dared to look up at the painting again.

This time, no Crazy Hezekiah. Instead, the space where Hezekiah was spotted was now replaced by the Wife of Bath. She was wearing a hideous smirk.

***

"Walk away, Ruth," I said as we finally sat in our usual booth in the corner. I had, as James requested, had my day of reckoning at the little chapel at a special time.

"What do you mean?" she asked with a beautiful smile. She wore a pretty red dress with small black polka dots. Two large braids that ran along the top of her smooth forehead met in a ponytail at the back of her neck and accentuated her glow.

"Walk away from the firm," I said, holding her hand in mine. "It doesn't deserve you."

"That's true, but—" she started. I reached into my left sports jacket pocket and squeezed a crimson box trimmed with old gold into her hand. "Ruth Hightower. Will you marry me?"

The silence that followed was unbearable. She looked down at the box and up at me, down at the box and at me again. I was conjuring up all the possible reasons she could or should say no. I was even preparing to forgive her, to somehow move on.

"I don't know what to say," Ruth said, staring down once again at the ring. Her eyes began to fill with tears. "All I've ever wanted was to be held by someone who loved me and cared. Yes! Yes, I'll marry you, Arnold Giovanni."

A month later she quit the firm, applied for and got a job at Ebonia College as public relations director. We married the next year on her birthday, November 11, at the campus main chapel. James was best man, and Brad and Bo Willie had practically begged to be groomsmen. Trent and Enoch rounded out the handsome group, all clad in black. The bridesmaids wore striking solid gold satin gowns.

Piper Jr., with a Nigerian middle name, and the cane and spitting image of his late father, had become theatre director at Ebonia College—English accent and all! As a favor to Trent, he superbly directed the wedding as if the party was a precision drill team. The history department faculty decorated the chapel throughout with rare flowers, along with the Egyptian mainstays of jasmine, hibiscus, mandrakes, chrysanthemums, poppies and bougainvillea.

Prior to Ruth's grand entrance, Piper Jr. set up a procession of 24 of the Chinaberry Tree's most ardent regulars, who strolled down the center aisle of the chapel with a resemblance to Chaucer's pilgrims.

Ruth's bridal gown was trimmed in gold and symbolic of an almost form-fitting, pleated kalasiris, with thousands of miniscule patterns likely crafted by a thousand partially blind seamstresses, along with an even more elaborate cocoon-like shendyt that left room for her decorated sandals. A headdress with horizontal stripes was braided into her hair and hung down between the blades of her shoulders. It was secured by a modius crown with the pseudo gold molds of seven asps, representing the seven continents.

Adding to her perfectionist's overkill were beaded collars with stones, mahogany and papyrus stems, golden hooped earrings and at least seven bracelets on each arm. Around her neck was a gold chain with a pendant in the shape of a chinaberry tree with seven branches. As she made her way to the front of the packed church and slowly ascended the platform, she placed a golden scepter on a stand designed only for that purpose.

When we finally exited the main chapel and walked into the cold November day to the waiting white limousine, the season's first snowflakes gently brushed our eyelashes and melted on our smiles. We were on our way to Addis Ababa to rediscover the roots of mankind and a good cup of coffee. The only world we had to be concerned about now would be the one we would create within Giovanni's room.

There remain so many stories to tell about the traveling spirits at The Chinaberry Tree, stories mired in the past and others vested in the visions of a world that is yet to be. And, even on what should rightfully be the happiest time in my life, I cannot shake those clandestine visits I had with Crazy Hezekiah, who, for whatever reasons, was not part of our wedding festivities.

One day, a final tale will capture the eventual and fiery fall of the empire of the present, leaving a gaping hole out of which will rise, like a phoenix, a chinaberry tree adorned with seven clusters. These were Hezekiah's murmurings. I had followed him secretly for so long that I could no longer, in good faith, call him crazy.

Each cluster of berries represents, he once proclaimed while sitting with his back to a sycamore tree in the park, a special gift presented by the old world to ensure the growth and strength of the new one.

Hezekiah described the first cluster as having 195 berries, denoting the countries of the world and their respective currencies that must be archived for history. Another cluster is made up of eight berries molded from a dying world's eight most precious metals. The third cluster of berries is redundant in that it not only represents the seven continents but the "keys" to safe places on each.

The smelly seer claimed that a fourth cluster features 10 berries representing the tentacles of the European Organization for Nuclear Research and its sisters around the world, originating in Switzerland and extending its luciferous arms into the U.S., Italy, Germany, China, Russia, Japan and other hidden locations, doing so in such a way as to defy the original sin. Each berry forms the other-worldly code that disables all operations around the planet that equate to playing God with high-energy particle physics experiments.

Hezekiah said a fifth cluster of 25 berries represents the 25,000 colleges and universities around the world and their research collusion with evil corporate interests that have skewed their missions. He called the institutions "anthills" that have ruined the green lawns of the earth. With the exception of Antarctica, Hezekiah prophesied that the day would come when each continent would be down to only 25 universities each.

Cluster six has six berries that will represent the six cities around the world that leaders from throughout the African Diaspora will meet before returning home to Israel in the seventh year, Hezekiah said to himself. The host cities for the six years will include Accra, Ghana; Washington, D.C.; Salvador, Brazil; Paris, France; Dubai, United Arab Emirates; and Sydney, Australia. Each international conference will end, he said, with participants conducting a march around the city's governmental center seven times. Finally, Hezekiah claimed that cluster seven boasts 54 berries, each symbolizing the 54 countries of the African continent, which will shed itself of Western pickpockets and control its own gold, platinum and diamonds, precious gemstones, industrial and base metals, rare earth elements, such as uranium and lithium, and many other minerals, leading to a slow but steady decline of the West necessary for the rebirth of empires.

The Roman courtier Petronius once said, "Heaven is equally distant everywhere." If every man on earth looked up toward the heavens, believing that far above him existed a higher power, then such belief places his world and his reality in the belly of that heaven. If heaven is above for the man at the north pole, as well as for the man at the south pole, then the earth must be engulfed by it.

Either way, I had been looking for a slice of heaven, and I found its essence in Ruth. Perhaps Ethel Mann was right: we often find what we are looking for. And, historian and Afrocentrist John Henrik Clarke once noted that, "Whoever is responsible for the hell in your life, is your devil."

What do you do when you come to realize that the only devil in the world might have sprung from a lineage too close to you? Well, you save yourself within the loins of Ethiopia, purging old empires and rebuilding all over again.

But I have listened to so, so many, and I have tried to decipher too, too many pieces in my desperate attempt to recapture my own lost soul. I pray that my own pilgrimage will continue to be nurtured by Ruth, and our family to come, launching an epiphany transcending all my wonderful past experiences and lessons. Most of all, I pray that The Chosen will find the truth revealed within every single berry of their own chinaberry tree.

The End

ACKNOWLEDGMENTS

My desire to write my first novel was inspired by James Baldwin, likely while I was a junior in high school. I attended the predominantly white Tuscaloosa High School in the late 1970s, and I was often smitten by any source of black art or literature that gained the respect of Southern whites. I also noticed how the choral conductor seemed enamored by William Dawson, the prominent arranger of Negro spirituals. Those instances led to my declaration of Baldwin as my favorite writer (to this day) and my decision to attend Tuskegee University, initially as an architecture major.

Two of the first people I opened up to about writing a novel were Geneva Southall at the Weaver Branch Library and Ammie "Lulu" Rutley Ward. Both were overwhelming supportive and one even arranged for me to acquire a typewriter. Nearly 50 years ago, I wrote a letter to Maya Angelou to let her know of my dreams. She was compassionate enough to write back: *"A 17-year-old James Baldwin? I certainly hope so!"* Of course, I have no idea what happened to that letter. It probably disappeared with the five rare dollar coins someone dared to hand me for graduation! I also wrote Nikki Giovanni that following summer, and she wrote back right away. I held onto the letter and presented it to her to sign again when she visited Tuskegee a year or two later. Well, you guessed it: I lost that letter, too.

I had a very rough draft of a totally different manuscript when I arrived at Tuskegee in late August of 1977. I mentioned it to my first roommate, Melvin Outen of Hempstead, New York. He immediately expressed interest and read every page of it in one sitting. After changing my major from architecture to English, I received a lot of inspiration and enthusiasm about Black literature from my professors at Tuskegee. I literally sat in every course offered by Dr. Loretta S. Burns! I remember visits by poets Samuel Allen and Rita Dove. Presentations by such notables as Vernon Jordan, Jesse Jackson, Marian Wright Edelman, Tony Brown, Carl Sagan, Sir William Arthur Lewis and many others became commonplace.

Yet, life happened over the course of five decades, and dreams were deferred. There were some bright spots, when I made some measurable gains on my project, but no completion. Those bright periods were often made possible by the ample assistance of colleagues Shirley Alexander, Linda Elliott and Debra Daniel. Then, after working in higher education public relations for more than 40 years, I finally decided to step away (much to friend Erskine McKinnon's chagrin) and to reclaim other interests, chief among them being my unfinished novel. The Lord works in mysterious ways, for had I met my last boss, Jamal Ali, just a year earlier, I probably would have worked at A&M even longer! We worked well together! Stephen McDaniel and Allen P. Vital, however, will always be the best bosses ever!

I am grateful to my supportive wife, Marilyn, and my wonderful daughter, Morgan, for their encouragement during those long, dry periods. Thanks to Dorothy W. Huston and Georgia S. Valrie (*alphabetically!*) for being among the best friends anyone could ask for. On the angels' side, there are my Episcopalian, Tuesday morning coffee buddies James D. ("Kappa") Foster, David ("True Irishman") Patterson and (sometimes) Leonard Hall and James Mitchell. Shout out to Richard Kelly, who could never make it! *(And that's too bad, because there have been too many inspiring conversations at Flint River Coffee Shop.)* The "good" side also includes the ladies of the "Worship Community Formerly Known as Holy Cross-St. Christopher's Episcopal Church": Karen Thiry, Marilyn Valberg, Pat Patterson, Brendlyn Hall and Gloria Benson. On the devil's side are my buddies Lamar A. Braxton, Jr., and LDAF, James W. Pope, Robert James Guice, Langdon Conaway and too, too many others to list. Right in the middle are Dr. Carla Clift, Dr. Annie Payton, the Harrison Center staff in Huntsville, and long-time Tuskegee friends Frank Lee and Carl Montgomery!

Finally, there are the beloved and extended family members of Web's Chaps (Linda, Johnny, Charles, Elaine, Helen, Lucky B and Aunt Ollie!) and the Ryans' set (Richard Ryans, dad; Eula Ryans, mom; Dr. Rosianna Gray, Eunice Prince, Timothy Ryans and Aunt Margie!).

Thanks to *every* person who had a role in making *The Chinaberry Tree* possible.

ABOUT THE AUTHOR

Jerome Saintjones is a native of Tuscaloosa, Alabama, where he grew up on Stillman Hill and first began his life of "paid" work solely for African-American entities. As a child, he helped to clean St. Paul Missionary Baptist Church on weekends. In junior high, he served as Student Government Association president and worked for Ida Glenn, a noted black piano teacher and graduate of the Oberlin Conservatory of Music. In high school, he participated in various organizations and worked afterschool for Stillman College as a dishwasher. Following his graduation from Tuskegee University, with the approval of Dr. Velma Blackwell, he worked in public relations at his Alma Mater for 10 years, followed by a year as assistant to the chairman (Frank H. Lee) of the Macon County Commission and then public relations specialist for the Southeast Alabama Sickle Cell Association, under the legendary Rosa T. Storrs. He was hired by historymaker Dr. Jeanette Jones as director of public relations at Alabama A&M University in 1992 and worked at that HBCU for 32 years, serving under seven administrators. In this capacity, Saintjones wrote thousands of articles, edited and designed numerous publications and even doubled as university photographer. His poetic talents span the penning of Tuskegee's Centennial Poem (1981) and the more recent writing of the school song (arranged by Andrea Bradford) for HBCU Drake State Community and Technical College in Huntsville, Alabama, under the dynamic administration of Dr. Patricia Sims. Saintjones has served since 2014 as the Senior Editor of *The Valley Weekly* (valleyweeklyllc.com), a popular online publication launched by longtime friend Dorothy W. Huston. The avid Episcopalian and his wife Marilyn Orange of Los Angeles (who served briefly as secretary for civil rights icon and lawyer Fred D. Gray) have one daughter Morgan, an advancement staffer at Alabama A&M University, where she is also a former Miss AAMU.

www.ingramcontent.com/pod-product-compliance
Lightning Source LLC
Chambersburg PA
CBHW020500310726
48979CB00016B/2743/J

* 9 7 8 1 9 6 6 5 1 9 0 0 3 *